ELLA
A STEPMUM'S TALE

J. L. HIGGS

BALBOA
PRESS
A DIVISION OF HAY HOUSE

Balboa Press books may be ordered through booksellers or by contacting:

Balboa Press
A Division of Hay House
1663 Liberty Drive
Bloomington, IN 47403
www.balboapress.com.au
1 (877) 407-4847

Print information available on the last page.

ISBN: 978-1-5043-0369-9 (sc)
ISBN: 978-1-5043-0370-5 (e)

Balboa Press rev. date: 08/11/2016

CHAPTER ONE

Sylvia Stark

"Are you ready, Sylvia?" my camera man, Stuart, asks, pulling me back from the daydream I was in.

"Yes, of course," I reply, plastering a smile on my face.

I am not really ready to do this, but then it is the whole purpose for us standing here in the cool breeze, in front of the large house, in the trendy leafy suburb of Daydreams.

Daydreams. What a strange name for a suburb! Maybe that is why it is so hard to keep my mind on the job...

No, there is more than that to my problems.

Deep inside I am tired of acting like a ditzy blonde with nothing more exciting in life than reporting on royal events and celebrity scandals.

When I left school I had wanted a more meaningful career, one that gets to the bottom of a story and not all this fairy floss, sweet and fluffy stuff.

That is not what is happening here though.

I look at Stuart and nod. His short brown hair is just showing from behind the camera, making it look like an alien mask. For a second the long lens becomes his nose but I force the image out of my mind. I can't get distracted again.

He is concentrating like the true professional he is. Boring. He has been married to the same girl, working for the same company, going through the same routine day after day, year after year.

Doesn't he ever get bored? Feel restless? I have to remember to ask him that after we finish here.

Here we go!

"Hello viewers and listeners, ABC Celebrity News Reporter Sylvia Stark here. It has often been said there are two basic stories that define the imaginary perfection of men and women."

"For men it is Superman, the ultra powerful male figure who saves the world against evil. He is rich yet humble, powerful yet caring, extremely handsome and yet not conceited."

"For women it's Cinderella, the lowly downtrodden young maiden who suffers the injustice of others with grace, never getting angry, always beautiful and yet also dignified".

"She embodies the ideal values of good, piousness, and ultimate virtue. It is a story that lives in almost every culture around the world to this day."

Slowly I walk up the driveway towards the house a few steps then turn around again, giving enough time for Stuart to adjust his equipment to keep up and then to scan the countryside.

It is pretty here. My soft pink suit with its tight short skirt fits in this formal setting perfectly. Too bad my blonde curly hair has a mind of its own. One small puff of wind and POOF! It leaps for joy in all different directions. I run my hand over it to bring a semblance of order before I continue.

Blah, blah, blah.

"Many listeners to this report will know how the story goes from childhood fairy tales but for those who missed out, I will give a brief overview."

"The story starts with Cinderella living with her widowed father, Henry Baker. Soon after the death of his wife, Susan, Henry remarries a woman named Charlotte Johansson. After a brief period of marital bliss he suddenly dies leaving Cinderella to be raised by her wicked and unjust stepmother, who dotes on her own two daughters."

"I have to remember to ask if she poisoned him or not! Oh sorry, the story continues."

"Cinderella is forced to do all the chores, the cleaning, sweeping and the cooking. Poor girl, no wonder she was so skinny! She had to wait on the rest of the household, all the while maintaining her sweet composure."

"I just want to give her a hug! She is so cute!"

"Anyway, one day the Crown Prince invites all the women of the countryside to a grand ball at the palace to choose his wife."

"For those of us lucky enough to be given the chance to report on the event, it was truly grand! Sigh! It was so romantic!"

"I could have danced all night. I wasn't really old enough to be there, of course. I'm not that old, really......Sorry, back to the story."

"However, the stepmother does not allow Cinderella to attend."

"The mean old cow. While home alone and almost giving up all hope, Cinderella is visited by a Fairy Godmother who temporarily transforms her into a vision of loveliness and transports her to the ball where she captivates the handsome prince."

"This is another thing I have to ask. Was this true?"

"Stuart, make a note of that please."

Stuart tells me to get back to the report.

"What? Get back? Get back to the report? Oh sorry, listeners, I seem to be easily distracted today. I do love a romance story."

I brush my hair out of my face and smile at the camera again.

I'm sure the viewers will think I don't have two brain cells left inside my head by the time I am through this performance. That was fine when I started out but I am over this charade. If the ratings were not so good I would shelve it in an instant.

"As the clock approaches midnight, she must rush home before the spell is broken and she returns to her shabby clothes. She only makes it to outside the palace walls before, poof! It all vanishes."

"The beautiful gown, the horses and carriage, everything gone!"

"I always feel like crying at this point! However, as she runs out of the palace she loses one of her glass slippers."

"Miraculously it is the only thing that doesn't vanish. The prince finds it and makes a lengthy search for her."

"Finally he comes to her house and when her foot fits the slipper and she pulls out the matching one from her pocket, the wicked stepsisters and stepmother are furious but it is too late. Serves them right."

"Cinderella and the Prince marry and live happily ever after."

"It is a theme about Good versus Evil where Good is always rewarded after many tribulations. It triumphs over injustice! It rises above adversities! Beauty conquers the Beast!"

"What did you say, Stuart? Get on with it? Oh, sorry, doing it again."

"Everyone should read and listen to the story of Cinderella, if for no other reason than to gain a deeper understanding of the underlying values and perceptions that shape our modern world."

"Now, ladies and gentlemen, boys and girls, I am outside the house of the Stepmother."

"Cinderella has been married for many years now and the wicked old lady is home alone, abandoned by her two daughters she has doted on to the detriment of our princess."

"It appears all her doting hasn't bought her daughters' affections."

"Serves her right. However in the pursuit of fair reporting, I have an appointment to discuss the story of her treatment of her stepdaughter with her. So, I am here to do the right thing. It is time to hear her side of the story."

I pause for a moment and watch Stuart.

"What's up, Syl?" he asks, lowering the camera from his shoulder.

I shrug my shoulders.

"Nothing. I just feel I am about to make the biggest mistake of my life. I'm going to need you to help keep me on track."

"Gladly," he says, smiling mischievously.

CHAPTER TWO

Mercilessly I plow on with my charade, flipping my hair, batting my eyelashes, swooning over images. My God, this is tough. What I wouldn't give for a real investigative story!

"As I walk up the pathway to the house, there is no indication a wicked stepmother lives here. The path is paved with a lovely warm shade of cream coloured pavers and lined with strawberries coloured roses. Hehehe. Reminds me of poor Hansel and Gretel. I bet the old witch had a fancy path like this."

"The house is large and elegant, made of beautiful creamy sandstone, two stories with high pillars, quite grand actually. Much better than the old house she lived in when Cinderella was growing up. I wonder how she could afford something like this? I bet she scrimped on the poor girl more than the story says."

A stone flicks me on the leg.

"OUCH! What are you doing, Stuart? Don't what? Oh, don't judge! Ah, of course. Sorry again. A reporter is supposed to be unbiased when conducting an interview even on a case as prominent and well publicized as this one."

"Charlotte only agreed to talk with me on the condition I ask reasonable questions and don't keep challenging her answers. I hope her answers are not too unbelievable then." Finally we have reached the front door. The moment I have been dreading is about to happen. Why am I so apprehensive? Of course we all know the answers I am going to get. That is what makes this so hard. It has all been told before in so many ways and in so many formats. Movies, books...ummm... movies, books.......

"Now is the moment of truth. I am knocking on the door. Can you hear that, listeners? I am using the solid door piece. Ohhh, it is shaped like a horse's head. How cute. I am knocking loudly. Knock, knock, knock. I like to do it three times for emphasis. For those who can't hear this because you are deaf or..... whatever.... It sounds solid, like I mean business. Not timid, like a tap, tap, tap."

"Just look at this view from the front door. How beautiful and peaceful. There is a lake at the bottom of the rolling green hill with a graceful white swan floating in it. She is obviously trying to copy the palace. The graceful driveway we drove up is threaded through a row of roses...It must be gorgeous when they are all in bloom."

I hear a mumble over my earpiece. Quickly I put my hand to my ear so I can hear it clearer.

"Shhh! Don't interrupt me, Stuart. I'm trying to describe my surroundings for the radio listeners. What did you say? The what is staring at me? Oh, the Butler! Hehehehe."

Quickly I turn around to face the tall slim stern faced man dressed in a formal black and white butler uniform.

"Greetings, sir, I... We have come for our interview with the wicked Stepmother.... Oh sorry..... with Charlotte Johansson Baker."

Silently he turns and steps to one side to allow us to enter the short entrance hallway. The closing door causes an echo and I nervously continue my report, keeping my voice as low as possible. I feel like an intruder even though we have an appointment.

"As we enter my first impression is the house is amazing with high ceilings, ornate architrave and even a cute white statue of a naked man. He really should have some clothes on. He must be cold. His strategically placed fig leaf is pretty small. Sorry kids, no porn for you."

"A sweeping staircase leads from the front foyer to the upstairs. The floor is white and grey marble and a grand chandelier hangs overhead. I sure hope that thing is secure. It looks heavy!"

"The Butler motions us along to our right. I'd love to explore this place but he has a stern look on his face. Clearly no wandering allowed. On the walls are beautiful prints of landscapes... wait.. they are not prints.... They are real paintings! She must have a lot money she hid from poor Cinderella!"

As I pause to admire the paintings, the butler motions us to continue walking. Why such a hurry?

"Now we are following the butler and we are shown to the drawing room. It is filled with dark leather furniture, soft creamy carpet and a lovely fireplace. The slight chill outside is nowhere to be seen or felt here. This is not what I expected at all! The rich earthy tones make the room feel warm and inviting instead of cold and scary like I thought it would be. The old scrooge was really holding out on our princess. I am getting quite cross while I sit here waiting for her to arrive."

Stuart puts his hand on my arm as he scans the room with the camera and squeezes tightly. It is all part of the play acting of our partnership that the public seems to love. What would it be like to do a serious interview? One of substance? Who really cares about the old Cinderella story anymore? I, for one, am over it. I pull my arm from his grip and pretend to rub it.

"Ouch! Stop that, Stuart! No pinching! Okay, I will try to stay positive and focused."

"The butler returns, bringing us a plate of cucumber sandwiches and little cupcakes while a maid carries in a pot of tea and coffee. My, doesn't she live well?! I bet she is trying to butter us up. I will not be bought even though they do look nice. Oh maybe I should have just one…. Oooh these do taste delicious. Maybe she is not as bad as the story makes out but where is she?"

I turn to look towards the door.

"I hear the sound of footsteps coming up the hall and the door opens to let a tall, slim lady dressed in a comfortable cotton frock enter the room. Her fashionably styled grey hair is hanging loose to her shoulders. If I didn't know better I would think I was sent to interview a cooking expert. Hehehe. Imagine that! Cinderella's stepmother actually knowing how to cook!"

Another mumble comes over the earpiece. Stuart is keeping me focused.

"Don't you threaten to turn off the recorder, Stuart. I have to give my opinion so the listeners can visualize what we are seeing. Humph! Too bad if you don't agree," I say softly. I stand up and plaster on a smile to welcome our host.

Thank you for giving us your time, Wicked Ste…. Sorry."

Quickly I close my eyes, put my head down then lift it up as if to start again and give my sweetest smile. "Charlotte."

"No problem at all. I apologize for keeping you waiting. I must admit I was surprised at your request for this interview. It has been many years since the story first broke, nearly twenty years I believe, and I have not been asked for my viewpoint for a long time."

"I have learned to live with the way my stepdaughter has told the story even though I saw it very differently. I suppose it will be nice to get my side of the story out in the public arena although I do not expect anything to change."

"At first I always declined anyone's request for information as I feared they would try to turn it against me. The questions were structured to bring out the worst possible answers. Things were pretty bad for a while. The Cinderella story has been very hurtful to me personally as you can imagine but the public seem to love it."

Her voice is soft and happy, not strict and sharp as I had been led to believe. Instead of any bitterness, the only emotional tone in her voice I can pick up is resignation. How bazaar!

Already I am feeling a little off balance and I haven't asked the first question yet. I glance over at Stuart to see his grinning "*I told you so*" face. How could he know? He is only a camera man not a reporter.

"How would you like to do this interview?" Charlotte asks after a moment of my staring at her in disbelief. She holds her composure well.

"I thought I would recount the story as we all know it and you can tell us your side," I reply nervously. "I prefer if you could give examples instead of just 'yes' or 'no'."

"That sounds like an excellent idea, my dear. I remember the only time I tried to speak up for myself the reporter asked 'Have you stopped beating your stepdaughter?' If I answered Yes, then it appeared like I had beaten her but stopped. If I answered No, it would appear I hadn't stopped when what I meant was I hadn't beaten her at all!" she laughs softly as she remembers.

"Please have a cup of tea before it gets cold. I may talk for hours so you will need to keep your strength up."

Wow! Caring, happy, relaxed? None of the descriptions I would have ever put down to describe the ultimate in Wicked Stepmothers. Just goes to show the importance of not being prejudiced. Yes, Stuart, I know.

CHAPTER THREE

I settle myself into the soft leather chair and try to look relaxed although I am prepared to bolt for the door at the first sign of trouble. I still can't be sure she won't suddenly change from this lovely polite lady into a hostile, horrible beast of a woman.

Stuart is standing to one side so he can move the camera back and forth as the interview progresses. Why does his brown hair always stay in place? He doesn't need to stay as tidy as I do but I have never seen a hair out of place. How does he do it? He must feel me looking at him so he looks up and smiles reassuringly.

Quickly I look away as he carefully connects a microphone to Charlotte's top so it will sit at the right position. I watch her facial expressions but I see no sign of a scowl. Instead I am the one frowning since I am really puzzled by her open friendly face. Is this really the woman I am supposed to be interviewing? She must have changed a lot over the years Cinderella has been away.

Stuart settles the camera on his shoulder and motions to me. Time to start.

"The first question I want to ask is 'Why did you marry Henry Baker? Was it for his money like the story says?'" I ask, expecting to catch her by surprise.

"The story goes you were a money hungry single mother who latched onto the lonely rich man with no thought of love." Stuart gasps but maintains his silence. He is rather noisy for a silent partner.

Instead of my question surprising her Charlotte completely surprises me when she throws her head back and laughs out loud and long.

"Oh no, my dear, no! We married for love and the sex was great."

"You only knew each other a short period of time before you married though," I protest. "How could you get to know him enough to love him in only a few months?"

"The length of time we knew each other makes no difference. Whether you are young or old, the hormones of sexual attraction can still be very strong. It is chemical lust that throws most people together so quickly. If it isn't there then you should not marry. The tricky part is staying together afterward."

"Don't forget, in those days it was not proper to have a romantic interlude outside of marriage nor were there any reliable contraceptives. If we had intercourse before marriage and I had fallen pregnant, the child would have been given up for adoption by a childless couple whether I agreed or not. Besides we had three children between us. It wouldn't have set a very good example for them either."

Looking at the lady opposite me it is hard to imagine her as a sexual being. Mind you I hate to think of my parents 'doing it' but they must have for me to come along. I shrug my shoulders hoping to remove the strange image of old people naked that flashed before my eyes. Ugh! I am glad the viewers can't see into my mind.

"I hope you don't get any more personal than that question," Charlotte says softly. "That is a bit harsh to start with."

I smile as I look at my note pad. The next ones are harsh as well. If she has a tendency to flare up, I want to catch it on camera. What great footage that would be! Proof of the harsh conditions our sweet Princess had to endure.

"What about the money though? Did you love him or lust for his money?"

I hold my finger up and glare at Stuart to keep him quiet. I have to ask these questions. The viewers and listeners of various programs over the years have emailed a large list of questions they want me to put to the Wicked Stepmother.

Besides, I find rich men a lot sexier than poor men. They exude confidence and know what they are doing! Maybe she felt the same.

Charlotte sits quietly for a moment watching the interaction between me and Stuart. I smile at her sheepishly, embarrassed at being caught having a silent disagreement with my partner.

It must not look very professional but, hey, this is a Cinderella Story. How professional do I need to be?

"I guess I had better address what you really seem most interested in. As for the money side of the question, have you ever heard of a Pre-Nuptial agreement?" she asks.

"Yes, of course. Did Henry make you sign one of those?"

I had never thought about that but it makes sense. Many celebrities insist on having one otherwise their serial marriage partners would leave them broke.

"No, my dear, I made him sign one. You see, I didn't need his money. He needed mine," she replies softly.

"He had this huge house and a huge debt to go with it. His last wife had accumulated large medical bills while she suffered from her various illnesses. We agreed that I would assist with the expenses we incurred together but he had to deal with the ones he had before our marriage."

I can see a flicker of pain cross her face as she remembers her dead husband. Does she still miss him? I want to ask her that but decide against it. It's not part of the story even though it would be interesting for an article on Grieving.

Even the most tumultuous relationships can be hard to get over if the spouse suddenly finds there is no one to nag.

Charlotte seems to have decided nothing is off limits and is tolerating me and my offensive questions a lot more than I deserve.

What? What am I thinking? She is the Wicked Stepmother! She doesn't deserve to be sheltered from the harsh reality of what she has done! She made the old man's life a misery! According to one story, that is. I sit and ponder this for a moment. I need more information.

"So what do you mean?" I ask.

"I would think it is completely obvious. He was broke. There was no money so there was no way I would have married him if I was only interested in his wealth. You know how I was accused of selling his precious paintings after his death?"

"Yes, that was going to be my next question. Why did you do that? Did you really spend it on your children and neglect Cinderella?"

She throws her head back and laughs out loud again. She is clearly enjoying this interview more than I am.

I am struggling to keep the story firmly in my mind since the answers to the first few questions have already unsettled me. Surely she hasn't been defamed for all these years?

Goosebumps flash over my skin as excitement races through my veins. I had never even considered the possibility she wasn't as bad as she was made out to be.

Maybe there is a real story here after all.

"If only I could have spent some on the children! Life would have been a lot easier," she says seriously. There is no sign of the laughter of a moment ago.

"No, it was to pay for his debts. His will stipulated that his goods should be sold to pay the various bills. It had been hoped by the time he died the bills would have been down low enough so it wouldn't be a burden on me and some of any money left over could be used to help raise Ella."

"So what happened?" I managed to ask.

I glance over at Stuart. He is watching Charlotte as if he is riveted to her, keeping the camera focused on her open honest looking face. This will make great viewing.

"I sold everything I could and when it was all gone, there was still a large debt left behind. The only way to pay them off completely was to sell the house but it was up to me whether I did this or not. I tried to keep it so Ella would have some continuity in her life. The poor girl had lost her father at such a young age."

"Ella? Don't you mean Cinderella?"

"No, I mean Ella. Her name is not Cinderella. The Cinder part came from the story of how she was dirty from cleaning the fireplace. That is only partly true as well."

"Oh, I didn't read that in my research."

Smiling softly at my comment, Charlotte stands up gracefully.

"I must step out for a moment. Please make yourselves another cup of tea."

I need a break as well. All this new information is really unsettling my preconceived ideas.

Maybe I should call this report 'The inconvenient truth about Ella'.

CHAPTER FOUR

Charlotte Johansson Baker

As soon as I am out of the room, I motion to Charles to join me in the study. He has been my butler, bodyguard, and support for many years now. No one would ever know he is also my younger brother and business partner.

"Charles, I am not sure about this woman," I whisper as I quickly log onto the computer.

"I want you to do a scan for any information you can get on her. The eavesdropping bugs hadn't prepared me for this kind of assault."

"Sure, Lotty," he replies. He seats himself at the computer and quickly types 'Sylvia Stark' in the search engine. "What have you got in mind?"

"Anything to indicate if I can trust her with the whole truth. I have to go back in there. If you find anything I need to know then feel free to interrupt."

"With pleasure. She has an interesting way of questioning."

"She does. I had expected someone a lot less pointed and probing. All I could find on her reporting style is fairy floss articles. This person in the drawing room is not what I expected *at all.*"

"It says here she graduated from high school with average grades but has an inquisitive mind. She got an apprenticeship as a reporter very young. Her first job was "The Wedding". She is two years younger than Ella. Wait!" Charles says as I am about to leave the room. "Her last boyfriend was arrested for drug dealing. *She* turned him in."

I muffle a laugh. "She is a tiger that one. A defender of truth. Maybe I need to give her some juicy information to sink her teeth into."

"I think she may be a good ally but are you sure you want to go through with your plan? Ella may not be ready yet."

"She is."

"Ok then. I'll keep looking for anything that would cause alarm bells and arrange for a team to plant the eavesdropper. What about her partner? Do you want me to check up on Stuart Fitzgerald?"

"No. Just her for now. I want to know everything I can about her. Put a tracker in her vehicle as well."

Returning to the drawing room where my guests are waiting, I plaster a smile on my face. I hate interviews like this.

I am not sure of how much of the truth to let out and how the Palace will react. When the whole story comes out it is going to cause a riot.

CHAPTER FIVE

Sylvia Stark

"So, my next question is about Henry. Did he die from a heart attack or not? I heard a rumor you may have poisoned him for his life insurance money," I ask, referring to my note pad.

"What really happened? From your viewpoint, of course."

"Of course," she says, picking up on my sarcasm. "My viewpoint happens to be the same one the medical profession holds as well."

"The heart attack part of the story is true to a point. Henry, as wonderful as he was, had a weakness for cream buns. Now that he had my help in covering the daily expenses he couldn't deprive himself of the small luxuries despite the doctors telling him how bad they were for him. He quickly gained a lot of weight and had just been diagnosed as a mature onset diabetic."

"Unfortunately the treatment then was not as sophisticated as it is now. It was only a matter of time before he had a heart attack or stroke with the way he was abusing his body."

"And there was no life insurance money as we couldn't afford to pay the premiums. Could you imagine the stories that would have appeared if I had taken out Life insurance on him then he died soon after! I would have been arrest or accused of arranging his murder!"

"Oh, that's right. That is why you just asked."

I shuffle uncomfortably in my chair. She is mocking me and my preconceived ideas. Most importantly she is mocking the naïve public who sent in these questions for me to ask. I need to be more objective but how?

I have lived with these ideas my whole life. I make a note on my notepad. Motive? None that I can see.

I cross off the next question. Someone had wanted me to ask if she felt guilty spending the Life insurance money on herself and her children. That is clearly no longer relevant.

Stuart moves the camera my direction so I smile into it and then back at Charlotte before I ask the next question on the list.

"Still on money matters, where did you get your money from once everything was sold?"

"I am sorry, Sylvia. I do not believe that is relevant to this interview. I only agreed to discuss those things related to Ella's upbringing and the numerous tales. That part is never in any Cinderella story so I view that information as too personal and irrelevant. The only thing I will say is that I have inherited some investments from my parents. It had nothing to do with my former husband who died suddenly in a swimming accident nor any insurance policies. That is enough about me. Please stick to our agreement."

She sits straighter in her chair with her hands clasped in her lap and raised eyebrows. I can imagine facing her as a disapproving school principal and I have faced plenty of them in my time.

Brr! Chills race up my spine. I would never want to be naughty in her school. I gulp nervously as I resist the impulse to shrink deeper into my chair. I guess I did overstep the conditions of this interview.

I am curious now though. What she is hiding? Did she do something illegal? I glance over at Stuart who is shaking his head in disbelief at my questioning. Looking down at the notepad I am relieved when I see the next question. Time to change direction.

"How did Henry get along with Cinder... Sorry, Ella?"

"How did they get along? Hmm, let me try to word this properly."

Charlotte stops to think for a moment, her sparkling blue eyes retreating through the years.

"How well does any child get along with a parent that never says *no* to anything she wants?"

"Great!" I say enthusiastically. I know I would have loved it if my father never said no.

"No, think about it. *Never* says *no*," she repeats, strongly emphasizing the idea.

I think for a moment before I reply, trying to put myself in such a position. I could have gotten away with so much more than I did. My poor parents would have been bald with pulling their hair out.

"Oh... I see what you mean! They try to keep pushing the boundaries and can become extremely spoiled and angry when they do not get what they want?"

I pause for another moment.

I'm not used to answering the questions. It takes time to think.

"It would only work as long as the child continues to get her own way."

"Precisely. That describes their relationship perfectly. I have been accused of doting on my girls but you have never seen anything like Henry and Ella. Heaven forbid, if he ever tried to stand up to her!"

"Can you give us an example?"

"Easily. I remember............Once upon a time."

"Henry, what is that white horse doing in the paddock next to yours?" I ask as we walk through the garden one day.

"It is Ella's new hack."

"I thought you got rid of the work horses because you couldn't afford to feed them any longer? That fine bred horse will be no use for pulling the carriage. Why did you get it?"

"She wanted it."

"She... She... Wanted... It? She is only twelve years old! Of course she wanted such a beautiful animal! How though, is she going to afford to feed it? Is she going to get a part time job in town? It would be good training if she had to work as a lady's maid!"

Henry looks away for a moment then back at me with tears in his eyes as he whispers "I have to find the money to feed it and care for it."

I sigh in frustration as I take both his hands and make him look me in the eyes. He is miserable.

"Henry dearest, we have been trying to work on a budget to get the expenses under control. That involves all of us making certain sacrifices. You can't keep spending money on her like this. Just last week you bought her another gown from the shop in town making it three this month! Why do you keep doing this?"

He sighs and finally admits. "I can't say no to her. When she looks at me with those beautiful blue eyes and flips her beautiful blonde hair, she reminds me of Susan before she died. I couldn't say no to her either."

"I can understand spending money on essential things like doctor's bills and electricity. But all the extra things have got to stop! Isn't that why you are in such a financial mess? You don't need to buy her things to show you love her."

He nods as his eyes tear up again. "I know I shouldn't. You are right. We can't afford all these things. Please help me."

"I am going to help you but I will not let you keep giving her everything she wants," I say as softly and lovingly as I can. "You must return the horse."

"I will lose money on it."

"If you discuss the circumstances with the previous owner I am sure he will be reasonable. Even if you lose a little it is better than having to come up with the ongoing costs of feed and vet bills."

The next day when Ella comes in from the front yard she storms straight past me without even saying good morning.

"Father! Where is my horse?" she demands. "It is not in the paddock."

"No, Ella, I tried to explain to you we can't afford another animal to feed and care for. One horse is enough and that is Emperor. He can pull the carriage as well as the plow," Henry says softly, looking up from his paper. "You can always use him if you need to go for a ride somewhere."

"How dare you?! That was my horse! It is that woman you married, isn't it?! She made you return it, didn't she?!" she says in a low growl. "I knew I couldn't trust you!"

"Well, your stepmother knows we can't afford it so she insisted I make the right decision. After all you got three new gowns this month as well. You really can't have everything you want, dear."

Ella glares at me and flicks her hair behind her back before storming off in a huff, slamming the door behind her.

"Yes, Ella got along well with others as long as things went her way," Charlotte says, shrugging her shoulders. "She never liked me from the first day but after that things just got worse."

"So Henry let her think it was your fault the horse was returned? That is not fair!" I reply, thumping my note pad in frustration.

She raises her eyebrows as she looks at me and smiles.

"Now, dear, this is why I want to tell my side. I must be fair though as it is not all Ella's fault either. Henry should have told her about the bills and the decision was his but then he didn't want to disappoint her. She had him wrapped around her little finger."

"What happened then?"

"Well, the new dresses she had managed to get were flaunted around the house for the next few weeks. She loved to make my girls feel unloved and to show she had won when it came to spending what little we had. After all she was her father's princess." She shakes her head sadly. "It was hard on us as I only bought dresses for my girls when they needed them. The only spoiled one was Ella."

"How often did you buy gowns for the girls? Were they always new?"

"Oh dear, no way could I afford new gowns all the time." She chuckles softly. "I taught the three girls to sew the best I could and we managed to modify second hand gowns our maid brought for us. Of course once she had to leave our employ, it was more difficult to get them. The girls, especially Ella, hated the idea of someone knowing they were wearing second hand dresses. We got very creative in turning them into very fashionable day garments though."

"Did only Ella get these second hand dresses?"

Charlotte looks at me for a moment then shakes her head.

"No, Ella was the tallest and oldest so often she got the new dresses then the girls got the hand-me-downs. That had to change when the girls caught up with her in height in their teen years. She hated it when she had to wear second hand dresses. She felt it was below her."

CHAPTER SIX

I don't like thinking of our beautiful princess as spoiled as her stepmother is making her sound. I have always known her to be gracious and loving, smiling to all of us lining the roadway to wave flags and tiaras as she goes past in the royal carriage. No, I will not accept this version of events.

"Surely the new gowns and horse was in payment for all the hard unpaid work she was doing around the house. If she thought your girls were getting new things, surely she was right to want it for herself?"

"Do you really think so?" Charlotte asks, raising her eyebrows. "I can assure you being a step parent is a hard job. I had to work hard at keeping everything equal so there was no sign of any favoritism."

"Can you give us an example?"

"Of Ella wanting the special treatment for herself only? There are plenty of them but I remember one time not long after Henry and I married."

Once upon a time............

"Henry, each of the girls has their chores to do before and after they go to school." I explain to him one day over lunch. "The tutor is

here at 10 o'clock each week day so there is plenty of time for them to get everything done."

"But Charlotte dear, Ella has never had to do chores before. Are you sure it is a good idea to start now she is nearly a teenager?" he asks. "When Susan was alive, she never made her."

"Yes, dear. Susan died when Ella was too small and not capable. Now she is growing up, she needs to learn to help around the house. One day she will want to marry or move out of home and at the moment she has no idea how to cook or clean or even sew. These are things Antoinette and Gabriella have had to learn since they were very young. It will be good for Ella to learn these skills too."

"If you say so," he says doubtfully. "Can't she just hire a maid to do it for her?"

"Henry, you know how bad your finances are. Ella has no idea how to manage money and will not be able to hire a maid unless she marries the prince. She needs to be a little bit useful around the house instead of relying on her looks. She has a brain so make her use it!"

"But…. does she have enough time? I don't want her to be tired before her studies. You know how much she struggles to concentrate when she is tired."

"Yesterday Antoinette and Gabriella got through their chores quickly and were at their desk waiting, on time, whereas Ella danced and sang instead of sweeping the floor as she was told. Henry, she refuses *to focus. She even told me there are mice in the holes of the cupboards who are her audience! She is a daydreamer and she needs to learn some discipline."*

"I didn't realise that."

"No I am sure you didn't. Of course the chores were not done in time so she was to do them after school. Not Ella though. She fluttered her long lashes at you and that was it. Do you remember what you said?"

"No."

"You said 'I know it is not fair, Ella. You shouldn't have to do all the work. Come on dear, come and have a chat with me. The other girls should do it, not you. You are my princess.' How do you think my girls felt?! They had already done their chores and now had to do hers as well! Plus you never saw the look of defiance she gave me as she followed you into the drawing room. She knows how to work you against me every time."

"I am sorry, my dear. I have never said no to Ella and she wanted to talk with me."

"Was it something important? If so, I can understand."

"No, I must admit it wasn't. She just wanted to complain about having to do chores."

"Henry and I rarely ever argued and when we did it was always over Ella," Charlotte says sadly as she brings us all back to the present. "It just got worse after his death. She became uncontrollable!"

"So are you telling me... us... Ella was spoiled by her father in every way?"

"Yes and I saw through it. That is why she resented me from the very beginning."

Referring to my notes in order to clear my head, I see the next line of questions need to be about the time of Cinderella growing up after Henry's death. It is obvious she had not liked Charlotte from the start and this is where the story of the Wicked Stepmother really takes hold.

After an insight into what the house must have been like before Henry's death I almost dread to ask about what it was like afterwards.

Still, there has to be some truth to the Wicked Stepmother and Evil Stepsisters story. Doesn't there?

At this moment the butler comes in so I have a sip of tea while he speaks with Charlotte. We have already taken an hour or more to get this far and I have hardly made a dent on the list of questions.

I probably should think about interviewing Ella to get her response now I have heard the other side of the story. Yes, that will be most interesting. Actually, I will take any excuse I can get to talk with the beautiful princess.

The butler continues to whisper something to Charlotte. The look on her face makes me wonder if the interview is going to continue.

She looks really worried. Has something happened?

Chapter Seven

Charlotte Johansson Baker

Charles comes up next to me and whispers in my ear.

"I found something. Not on her but on Stuart. He used to be a special arms soldier for the palace guards. One of the King's elite bodyguards."

I try to keep the surprise from showing on my face. Is there a spy in the ranks?

"There's more. He is married to the daughter of the current Palace Commandant. If you are not prepared to go through with your plan you had better pull up now."

"That will be all," I say softly to Charles, putting my hand on his arm.

He knows what that means. I need to go ahead with the interview. The timing is right. I can't pull up even if I wanted to.

Sylvia refers to her notes for a moment.

My answers are obviously not what she has expected but she is managing to hide her surprise well. She turns to face me as soon as Charles moves away to stand to one side.

"The story goes that after Henry's death you made Cinderella do all the housework and serve you cups of tea in bed. She had to do all the cooking and cleaning while your daughters did nothing. It also goes that she had to wear rags instead of good clothes. What do you say about *that*?!" she asks with a little too much force.

Stuart kicks her with his foot to pull her back in line. I hide my smile behind my hand and try to look upset by the question. He is a lot more disciplined than she is but my respect for her is growing. She is not afraid of anything.

"Oh dear, I can hear in your voice you are not very happy with the answers you are getting. Are you sure you want to continue the interview?" I ask kindly.

After what Charles told me I want to make sure all those in this room are up to the task I have planned for them.

If Stuart is a rabid royalist spy then things could get tricky.

She looks chastised for a second but I can see the battle of her emotions playing across her face.

She is obviously a reporter with passion for finding out the truth even though the answers are not what she expects. Once she is convinced of what really happened she will be a force to reckon with. I just need her on my side.

She takes a deep breath to settle her emotions before she continues.

"I want to continue the interview. I apologise, Charlotte. Please let me rephrase the questions. The story goes that after Henry's death, Ella was turned into a servant. Is that true?"

"Let me ask you some questions first, Sylvia. In the movies and story books, where is Ella always pictured and what is she doing?"

I watch her closely as she answers. I want to see how fast off her feet she is. Can she cope with being in the spot light?

"In the kitchen, cooking or cleaning."

"Yes, in the kitchen. Now what do you know about the house she grew up in?"

"It was huge."

"That it was. It had ten bedrooms, five other rooms and five bathrooms other than the kitchen. If Ella had to do all the work, don't you think she would have been pictured in another room occasionally?"

"I don't understand."

"It is quite simple really. All the rooms needed cleaning which included sweeping, mopping and putting things away. Antoinette, Gabriella and myself did all the other rooms, leaving Ella to care for the kitchen and her own room. She definitely didn't have to clean *everything*." I laugh softly. "If I had insisted on her doing any more than that she would still be on the first room after all these years!"

"What do you mean?"

"I am not sure how to say it any other way. Ella was a day dreamer. When she was supposed to be sweeping she danced around the room with the broom, sweeping nothing. When she was supposed to be dusting, she pretended the duster was a wand. Like I said before, she was always performing in front of her imaginary mice audience. It caused a lot of arguing. The kitchen was always such a mess. At least the other rooms were tidy in case we ever had visitors."

"So.... Tell me more."

"Well, after having to remind her numerous times to get on with her job, she would eventually get it finished. The girls offered to change jobs with her because they felt the kitchen may have been too big for her. I wouldn't let them as I was trying to teach Ella to be a tidy cook."

"So did she have to care for the cooking all by herself?"

"Again I ask you to think of what the movies and books show? There is always a large pot of potatoes she has just finished peeling and pots and pans piled up high in the sink ready to be washed. How many people do you know that only eat potatoes every day?"

"Not many," she admits reluctantly but I can see her opposition is crumbling more by the minute. "So what are you trying to say?"

"After Henry died, I could no longer afford the cook so the meals had to be prepared by myself or my girls while Ella daydreamed of having maids. Ella thought she did everything and that is what she told anyone who would listen but in reality she did very little other than complain. She took four hours to peel that pot of potatoes where a normal person would take only one! The mess she left behind is hard to describe. She had spread peelings from one side of the room to the other. Even the ceiling had peelings as she waved the knife around like a wand. I won't even comment on the condition of her own room!"

I pause for a moment to make sure Sylvia is following me. So far so good. I glance at Stuart. He seems like he is caught hook, line and sinker. Yes, I do believe I have two media personnel ready to join my team. Just a few more steps.

"That was all we could ask her to do otherwise dinner would never be done on time. It was very hard to keep calm with such a difficult child. She may seem to be peaceful under persecution as the story goes but in reality she was the epitome of the dumb blonde. She couldn't do more than one task at a time and even that was a struggle."

"That is being a bit harsh, don't you think?" she protests. "If you had as much money as you indicated then why didn't you hire a maid?"

I shrug my shoulders as I lay the foundation for the battle lines.

"Maybe I am the wicked stepmother after all!"

CHAPTER EIGHT

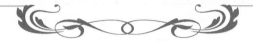

Sylvia Stark

I need to keep following the story line angle of questioning. There has to be something that is true here somewhere.

"What about serving you breakfast in bed? Didn't she do that?"

"Yes, she did it once and it was very nice. I was really surprised at first."

I jerk my head in surprise. At last, something is true!

"What do you mean 'at first'?"

"She wanted to go out to a dance with the local girls and she knew she had to start doing a few nice things if she was going to get any privileges. I was informed of her conditions before I took the first sip of the tea."

"Did she go? Or did you forbid her to go anywhere?" I ask doubtfully.

Of course she was forbidden to go. Cinderella was always forbidden to have any fun.

"Yes she went."

Another surprise! She couldn't have gone. Not according to the story.

"What? I thought she wasn't allowed out of the house?" I ask, suspicious she is not telling me the whole truth.

One of them has to be lying. Surely not the Princess!

"Sylvia, I am hoping by now you are starting to see there is another side to this story. Personally, I feel sorry for all step mothers. They are damned if they do and damned if they don't."

"Why? What happened?"

"Ella came back very early in the morning and refused to say where she went after the dance finished but I could tell she had too much to drink. She had gone missing for several hours and I was very worried about her safety."

"Oh." My heart sinks.

Our princess was a delinquent.

"Remember she was sixteen years old by this time. She was still a minor, especially in those days."

I hesitate for a moment, trying to get my thoughts together.

"So was she confined to her room after that?"

"I did put her under some restrictions. She was not allowed to go out by herself for some time until she could prove herself trustworthy and when we went anywhere together as a family she had to come home with us."

Charlotte chuckles. "I planted a rose bush under her window. That was the only way to keep that girl in at nights until she moved to the tower."

"I want to ask you about the tower later but back to her being allowed out," I say, making another note on my pad. "What about the clothes? Did she have to wear ragged clothes around all the time? I know what you said about the ball gowns but what about her day clothes?"

Charlotte laughs loud and hard.

"I do so wish we had the fancy cameras back then like we do now!"

"Why? Were they not rags?"

"Oh, yes, they were ragged. And yes, she was dirty. But it is only because she refused to put her clothes away in the cupboards."

"Please explain."

"Each of the girls got a new dress as they grew and as I said they also wore second hand dresses we modified but these were mostly for around the house. I tried to make the money I had before I married Henry last as long as possible but I still wanted the girls to look nice. I do mean all three girls."

"Ella thought it was below her to put her clothes in the washing machine and refused to learn how to mend a tear or replace a button. She expected one of us to go into her room and tidy it up for her. Of course that was not going to happen."

"Finally she ran out of clean clothes and started to complain about having nothing to wear but rags. I took her into her room and explained if I find a single piece of clothing on the floor I would confiscate it. She was not going to get any different treatment than the other two. We had no maids so if we didn't do it ourselves then it didn't get done. She had to wash, iron and mend her own clothes just like the rest of us but she flatly refused."

"I gave her one week to at least get started but there was no attempts made whatsoever. She didn't believe I would take them but I did. I loaded them into a bag and stored them in a trunk in my room. Eventually I cleaned and repaired them and then gave them to the other two girls. So while my girls were wearing nice clothes, she had to wear her rags."

"You didn't give in even when she got covered by the soot in the chimney?" I ask. "Surely she needed something to change into while she washed her rags?"

"Sylvia, the girl's whole problem was that people kept giving in to her. She could have worn a shift over the top of her dress, just like we all did when it was our turn to clean the chimney. No, she wanted to play the situation for as much sympathy as she could get."

"Who would give her sympathy if no one knew?"

"Ah, we had visitors later that same day. Her friends from the dance came by so of course she had witnesses to how bad I was treating her. A bit convenient, don't you think?"

After a moment the only thing I can thing to ask is "She had friends visit?"

Cinderella was supposed to be alone and in servitude. Having friends visit? That wasn't part of the story.

"Yes but not very often. It didn't take long before they saw what was really happening."

"Oh!"

Seeing events from the other side is sure putting a different slant on things.

CHAPTER NINE

"Let's move on to how she got along with her two step sisters," I say as I clear my voice.

This interview is definitely not what I expected. I wonder what I will find here in this category of questions.

"How did they treat her?"

"Antoinette was the more outgoing of the girls and only a year younger than Ella. She couldn't stand Ella's attitude and her sense of entitlement. Don't forget my girls had already lost their father a few years earlier so Ella could have had close friends who empathized with her if she had not behaved so badly."

"Can you give us an example of this?"

"Oh yes. I remember one situation quite clearly."

Once upon a time.................

"Charlotte!" Ella screams. "Netty has taken my gold brooch!"

I hurry from my room to see the two girls tugging over an old gold brooch that used to be my mother's. I had offered to let Ella wear it with a gown she had on once but I had made it clear to her she was to give it back. Still I hadn't pursued its return and it had been several months.

"It isn't your brooch, Ella. It is my grandmother's!" Antoinette says firmly and coldly. "You only borrowed it. Now I want to wear it. Mum said I could."

"No, she gave it to me!"

"No, she didn't!"

"Yes she did!"

"Stop!" I yell over the top of their voices. "Give it to me!" The two girls stand glaring at me and each other while I hold out my hand for the brooch. "Now, Ella! Hand it over." Reluctantly she slaps it into my hand. I feel a sharp sting from the pin and quickly withdraw my hand. The pin has caused a drop of blood appear.

"That is not fair. You gave it to me now you are taking it back. I don't have anything of my own!" she pouts, crossing her arms in front of her and slumping her shoulders. Tears start streaming down her face making her look so young and pathetic. "I wish my father was here."

Antoinette sighs sadly. I know she is still grieving the loss of her father and she is very sensitive to the feelings of others.

She starts to say "I miss my dad too, Ella....."

"I am not talking about you!" Ella snaps angrily, wiping the tears from her face. "If my dad was here he would make her give it to me!"

Antoinette looks as if she has been slapped in the face. Her cheeks turn red and tears spring to her eyes as she turns away to hide the pain showing on her face.

"She understood what it was like to miss a beloved father and to feel really insecure in yourself but that wasn't the reason Ella missed Henry." Charlotte sighs sadly.

"Antoinette avoided Ella for as long as she could after that. Netty had loved her father, Richard, and she tried to love

Henry for the brief time we had him with us. However Ella made our lives such a misery."

"What about Gabriella?" I ask softly.

I can just imagine the turmoil in the household. All that female emotion swirling around with no outlet! Volatile!

"How did she and Ella get along?"

"Gabriella was much quieter than Antoinette and a peacemaker. I had to keep an eye on her and Ella all the time."

"Why?"

"Gabby wanted to make everyone happy so Ella could easily get her into trouble if I didn't stop her."

"Do you have an example?"

"Oh yes. You won't like it though," Charlotte warns.

Once upon a time........

The three girls and I walk into the HD Ballgown shop in town, looking for something special for each of them. It had to be suitable as they were going to the ball celebrating their last year of schooling.

It is a Debutante Ball and it is to be held at the Palace, a first for the girls, so they are very excited.

"What beautiful gowns!" Netty whispers in awe as she walks around, unsure of which ones to look closer at first.

Ella has her eye on the gown in the window. It is white and sleeveless and very form fitting, leaving very little for the imagination to fill in. "I want that one!" she says firmly.

When I see the price tag I would have swallowed my false teeth if I had any. It was double the price range I had given the girls.

"I am sorry, Ella," I whisper politely. "Look at something else. You don't even know if it will suit you."

"No!" She insists. "I want that one!"

"Ella. I said look at something else. That one is too immodest for a young lady to wear. Your breasts will fall out of it when you try to dance!"

She huffs herself up in preparation of making a scene when the sales lady comes from the back of the store. Suddenly she smiles and flutters her eyelashes.

"Of course, Stepmother," she says sweetly. "Whatever you say."

I roll my eyes in exasperation. I have seen this performance many times before.

After a while I find one much more suitable for a girl of her age so I look around for her. Even though it is just over what I had been prepared to spend, I decide that if she likes it I will buy it for her. After all, she is growing up into a beautiful young woman and this dress should be the last one before she starts buying them for herself.

I finally hear two girls giggling in the change room. It is Ella and Gabby.

"What are you doing in there?" I ask.

"Nothing," Ella responds quickly and the giggling stops. Immediately I know they are up to something.

"Come out of there at once!" I demand, knocking on the change room door.

Gabby and Ella come out with Gabby's backpack suspiciously bloated, still sitting on the ground.

"What have you got in there?" I ask Gabby. She doesn't answer but looks down and blushes. She is a hopeless liar.

"Nothing!" Ella says firmly. "We are ready to go now. There is nothing I like here."

She picks up the backpack and hands it to Gabby but I grab it before she has a chance.

Quickly I open the bag and take out what is inside. It is a beautiful white sleeveless gown, the same as the one on display in the window."

I stare at Charlotte as what she is saying falls into place.

"She tried to steal a dress?"

"Yes." Charlotte nods. "She actually tried to get Gabriella to do it for her."

"Did she succeed in stealing anything that you know of?"

"She managed to steal the glass slippers the next year and I am not sure how she got the gown she wore. I know I didn't buy it."

"What! Do you mean *the* gown? The one she claimed the Fairy Godmother gave her?"

My mouth has dropped open in shock making it hard to speak. I can't *believe* what I am hearing!

Charlotte smiles sadly and nods.

"Yes, Sylvia, I believe the gown and the glass slippers came from the same shop. That is the real reason she had to leave in a hurry. The shop keeper, Mrs Dumpt, was at the ball as well and recognized the outfit."

Stunned, I stand up in a daze and manage a weak smile.

"I am sorry. I am going to have to stop the interview here."

"I understand. I am so sorry, Sylvia."

Charlotte shakes her head, looking down at her hands before looking up and continuing softly. The sadness in her voice adds to the shock. She feels sorry for me!

"It punches at the very core of the image she has tried to portray. Now you understand why I haven't said anything over all these years."

Silently Stuart and I pack up the camera and microphones and head for the front door while Charlotte watches us. Stuart is just as shocked by the revelation as I am.

"I am sorry to upset you so much," she says softly before we leave. "I haven't spoken about this for so long I guess I forget how bad it sounds when spoken out loud."

"Please don't get upset with Ella or the Prince over what I have said. I don't want any backlash."

The butler shows Stuart and I out of the house while Charlotte remains sitting in the cozy room. I am in such a daze I don't even think of pausing to look around at the beauty of the place. I just need to get out of here and back to some kind of reality. It is like I have been transported into an upside down world.

What is real? Is everything I knew and believed all wrong? Is Cinderella really a delinquent? Next I'll find Superman is on steroids.

As soon as Stuart and I have everything loaded in the vehicle I get in the passenger seat and wait for him to drive us back to the studio. Normally I would fight him for the keys but not this time.

"Stuart, did you get all that on record?" I ask softly.

"Yes," he replies. "Every word of it."

"What do you think we should do?"

He shrugs his shoulders.

"I think we need to interview the Princess. These allegations are pretty damaging to her reputation. We can't use the footage unless we get it verified."

I nod in agreement.

"This is going to be one helluva fairy tale."

CHAPTER TEN

Normally getting an appointment with the Royal Princess is not very easy so I am surprised and relieved when her secretary calls me back within an hour.

She has agreed to give a response to Charlotte's interview. The appointment is set for two days' time.

I have to wait *two days* before the contradiction to the Cinderella story can be cleared up.

I know it has to be a misunderstanding here. Surely a clear and logical explanation will prove the Wicked Stepmother is indeed wicked and the story I love so much will be firmly established as the truth.

After all, the dreams of so many young girls hinges on it, doesn't it? If Charlotte has told the truth, then who will the girls look up to? A selfish, scheming girl who is too lazy to work?

A delinquent with a major 'sense of entitlement' disorder?

No! That can never happen! I have to find a way to establish the equilibrium again.

Driving up to the Palace is usually a special experience. You can see the whole country from up here.

We are a small country but from the Palace we can see Daydreams at the base of the hill, all the way out to Flanagan which is an hour's drive to the east. Between the base of the hill and Flanagan are the hills of Soho Heights (where the home of Henry Baker still stands) and the City of Soho itself. Royal Valley, where our studio and offices are, is also based at the bottom of this hill slightly to the west of Daydreams. From here each township looks defined, beautiful, and elegant.

The Rhyme River snakes its way from Flanagan, through the countryside and into the lake behind the Palace. The still water of the lake is vibrant with silhouettes of the beautiful trees on its shores.

As we enter the Palace grounds the road way is lined by white roses and green lawn, set off by the white gravel. Normally the beauty of the place would bring tears to my eyes.

However, my brain is still out of balance after having gained an insight into the other side of the Cinderella story. The shine seems to be missing.

Standing in front of the large wood doors set in a white marble frame normally sends goosebumps up my arms.

Today, though I feel a sick lump in my stomach.

Even the amazingly elaborate door hammer in the shape of a crown on a lion's head does nothing for me.

Everywhere I look things are overdone in grandeur and expense.

Stuart is still giving me the 'I told you' look as I connect the microphone to my shirt collar and prepare to knock on the door. I need to ask him what he is really trying to tell me.

Is he telling me not to believe what I have been told? Not to believe my dreams? What can I believe then?

"Ready?" I ask as I put the microphone in a more comfortable position. "Uh uh hum. Sound check. Okay, ready."

I look up and into the camera Stuart has pointing at me, trying to put on the airy happy personae the viewers expect to see when tuning into our program. I just hope no one notices my eyes are not convinced by the charade.

"Welcome Viewers and Listeners. We are standing outside the front door of the Royal Palace in preparation of getting Cinderella's side of the story. We all know the much publicized story we have come to love and to trust but after hearing from the Stepmother, a number of issues have been raised. For example, was Ella really as hard done by as she claims? Was she as spoiled as Charlotte claims? And did she *really* steal *the* dress?"

"*Cut!*"

I shout as I step from in front of the camera, putting my hand to my head. I can't believe I am about to do this. Can I really call the Princess a liar?

"Stuart, can I ask her questions like that?"

"You asked Charlotte if she married Henry for money so there is no reason you can't ask the same pointed questions to Ella," he says. "If she stole the dress she needs to confess regardless of whether she is the Princess or not."

I shake my head to clear my thinking. It all feels so wrong! If what Charlotte says is true, then the world has lost a hero, a role model, even an icon.

"Okay, let's get this over with," I say, stepping back in front of the camera and plastering a smile on my face.

"So viewers, I am knocking on the door. Knock, Knock, Knock! *Cut!*"

I call again. "Stuart, that sounds too corny. I really don't want to do this."

"Sylvia, you are a news reporter. You report the news," he says kindly. "Do your job. You have a breaking story here. This has gone beyond the typical Cinderella story. You have to find out why there are so many inconsistencies in the two sides. There may be a simple explanation to all of this."

"Okay," I sigh. "Let's do this."

A butler dressed in a formal black and white uniform opens the door, closely followed by two guardsmen dressed in red and gold uniforms and armed with guns.

I would have expected swords instead, seeing they are dressed in such old fashioned uniforms.

My attention turns back to the butler. His straight posture seems almost unnatural. I wonder if his uniform is so severely starched it won't bend.

I can't help comparing him to the one we met at Charlotte's house. That one seemed much more human even though he never spoke to us. His eyes sparkled with interest in what was happening around him.

This one seems to have difficulties meeting my eyes.

Immediately I think of the figurine I have at home of three frogs sitting on a log 'Hear no evil, See no evil and Speak no evil'.

Is that what goes on here? Does he turn a blind eye to corruption?

"We are here for our appointment with the Princess," I say as I give my sweetest smile.

The butler leads the way while the two guardsmen follow close behind. We are shown through the immense entrance foyer into a grand room full of gold and marble statues and a few pieces of expensive but uncomfortable looking lounge chairs.

It makes Charlotte's amazing house look mundane.

It is the Royal Palace after all. I look around in awe but a small niggling doubt keeps eating at me.

Had Ella planned to marry the Prince like Charlotte implied?

Was it all planned so she didn't have to work?

Stuart and I stand by our chairs as we wait for her Highness to join us.

When she sweeps gracefully into the room I catch my breath. She is absolutely beautiful, dressed in a soft blue gown and wearing a small tiara in her expertly coiffed blonde hair.

She is the perfect picture of grace and elegance.

Surely, Charlotte wasn't telling the truth!

As soon as she sits down, I sit in my seat staring at her while Stuart arranges the microphones and camera.

Wow! What a privilege to be interviewing Cinderella!

My heart is racing and nerves are making the paper on my lap shake so much it is hard to focus.

No one gets this close and personal with Cinderella. I sure hope I don't stuff this interview up!

"Princess Cinderella, I suppose the first question I should ask is what your real name is?" I ask, taking out my note pad so I can check the answers to each question. "What should I address you as?"

"What a most unusual question. Why do you ask?" She seems genuinely surprised to be asked such a question.

"Your stepmother said your real name is actually Ella. The 'cinder' part was added to emphasize the dust you got on your clothing."

Her lips purse together for a moment as if she is unsure of how to answer. I would not have thought that was a trick question. Surely she knows her own name!

"That is true," she finally replies. "My name is not Cinderella but just Ella. You may call me Princess Ella."

"Thank you, Princess Ella," I say, sighing with relief. The first question is over.

"The questions I want to ask are in response to the information I gained from your stepmother during an interview I conducted with her last week. I mentioned this fact at the time of asking for this appointment but I want you to realise I do not necessarily believe the answers I got at the time are true. That is why I am here. I want your response to these allegations before we use them in an article or on the Celebrity show."

She graciously nods her head and raises her elegantly gloved hand to indicate to proceed. Wow! She is so beautiful.

"Okay, the next question is regarding your relationship with your father," I say clearing my voice. "How well did you get along with him?"

"He was a wonderful man. I miss him deeply," She replies, with a sad look on her face.

"Yes, I understand he was, but how well did you get along with him? Did he ever say *no* to you as a child?"

Again Ella purses her lips as she considers how to answer. She looks like a fish puckering up to kiss the side of the fish bowl. Or maybe she is puckering up to kiss a frog. No, that last one is too weird.

"He was a wonderful father before Charlotte came along," She says. A touch of bitterness creeps into her voice.

"Yes, I understand he was but how well did you get along with him? Did he ever say no?" I repeat.

I am starting to believe Charlotte since I can see how hard it is for Ella to give me a straight answer.

"He didn't say no unless she made him," the Princess replies. "We never argued until she came along."

"Is that because he never said no to you?" I persist. "Were you spoiled?"

"I am unable to answer that question," Ella says firmly. "I was only a child. I cannot remember any particular account."

I place a tick against the answer Charlotte gave me. Henry never said no.

CHAPTER ELEVEN

A maid wheels a trolley with a teapot and cups into the drawing room so we pause with our interview to enjoy some refreshments.

As the Princess quickly stands up and leaves the room without saying a word, I glance over at Stuart. He raises his eyebrows and shrugs his shoulders.

What is that reaction for?

Have I upset her with only two questions?

She is only away for a brief moment. When she returns to sit in her throne-like chair, I glance down at my notepad and prepare to ask another question.

"Princess, I would like to ask you about how you got along with your stepmother. Did she make you do all the jobs in the house like the story goes?"

"Yes, of course," she says softly.

"Who cleaned the other rooms while you worked in the kitchen?"

She sits quietly for a few minutes. Her eyes and facial expressions are completely blank. I can't read any emotions or body language coming from her.

"I can see what you are doing, Ms Stark. You are trying to undermine my reputation. I do not appreciate this."

"It is a simple question, Princess," I reply, putting my hand on top of my notepad.

If she could only see the other questions I have planned for her, we would get kicked out. I am really surprised at the tension in the room.

She sighs and leans back in her chair as if resigned to answer a very difficult question of life or death.

"My stepmother and stepsisters did help a little," she admits.

"So the story that you did *everything* isn't true, is it?"

"No," she whispers.

A guardsman comes up to her and whispers something in her ear. It takes only a few seconds before she turns her attention back to us.

"I feel the interview is not going to be very successful if you insist on your line of questioning in front of a camera. Please submit the questions you wish to ask to my lawyer," she says, passing a business card to me. "You may leave now."

Suddenly she stands up and sweeps out of the room graciously and fully poised, leaving Stuart and I stunned.

We had only asked three questions and I cannot see what is wrong with them. Surely the stepmother's side of the story isn't true after all?!

The guardsman comes to escort us off the premises so I help Stuart pack up the camera and microphones and we hurry to the car.

As soon as we finish and head down the drive, I look to Stuart.

"What just happened?" I ask him.

"I think you hit a raw nerve," he says as he negotiates the car onto the busy highway. "She couldn't take the pressure. What do you want to do now?"

What do I want to do? Hide? Run? Quit my job and travel to a remote tropical island? No, this might be what I have been looking for.

"Let's go back to the office and prepare the list. I want to visit the lawyer as soon as possible. I feel there is something about this story that the public needs to hear about. Something is not right and I want to find out what it is."

Thump!! Suddenly we are hit from behind with a heavy thud, sending our car fishtailing out of control and across several lines of traffic.

"Hang on!" Stuart shouts as he struggles to regain control of the car.

I look behind to see a large black four wheel drive hummer coming at us again. Stuart must see it as well. He jerks the car to one side and heads for the exit just as it clips our tail end, sending us sideways. Stuart pulls heavily on the steering wheel and just manages to get the car straight again when suddenly we hear a sharp crack. Our rear window shatters.

"Someone is trying to kill us!" I scream, hanging on to the dashboard to keep from being thrown around.

"We have to pull over," Stuart says firmly and in a lot more control than I am feeling.

I look over at him and see blood seeping from his right shoulder.

"You have been hit!"

"Yeah, I know. Help me steer into that car park behind the supermarket."

I grab the steering wheel while he tries to stop the bleeding. The pain must be intense. I hope he doesn't faint on me. If both of us faint who will drive the car?

Together we manage to navigate between two large storage containers. Hopefully the ones chasing us haven't seen where we are hiding. No one should be able to see us unless they were watching. I grab a towel from my makeup kit on the back seat and hand it to Stuart.

Blood is pouring out, staining his white shirt. He is struggling to get out of his seat belt so he can loosen his jacket enough to reach the wound.

"How bad is it? We have to get you to hospital," I say as I try to help him hold the towel over the wound.

"We have to deal with our visitors first," he whispers, staring out of the front windscreen.

His face is pale and sweat is breaking out on his forehead as shock sets in.

I sit back and follow his gaze.

There in front of us are two heavily armed men dressed in swat clothes. Have we landed on a movie set? These guys look like paid assassins. Quickly I look behind and see two more approaching from behind.

"Stay in the car," I whisper.

According to office rumours, I am supposed to be able to talk my way out of any situation but this is the first time I have been on the wrong end of a gun.

My nerves are flying wildly.

As I wiggle my way out of the car, I realise parking between two immovable objects wasn't such a good idea after all.

The door doesn't open all the way and it limits our ability to escape. Wearing a tight skirt is not such a good idea either when trying to negotiate my way out of the tiny slot the door gives me. I have to pull it up *way* too high in order to get out.

Well, I wasn't planning on this happening, was I? I would have worn overalls if I had known. What am I thinking?

"What is going on?" I ask firmly as I straighten my skirt. I hope the men behind the car didn't get a view of my underwear.

How embarrassing to be caught out on the day I wore my granny undies. Pretty lacey ones might have given me more sympathy.

"We are reporters, not terrorists. I am Sylvia Stark of the ABC Celebrity News and the one you shot is my camera man."

"We know who you are," one of the men growls. "You can take this as a warning."

"Some kind of warning!" I protest, getting my nerves under control. "A warning against doing what?"

"Against harassing our Princess."

Suddenly the men turn around and disappear to the other side of one of the large containers. As I stand clutching the door of the car, I can hear the roar of the hummer as it leaves the car park.

Stunned, I wiggle my way around the car and open the driver's door.

"Shift over. I am going to drive you to hospital."

As I carefully back out of our tight spot and head for the hospital, I glance at Stuart. He is frowning.

"Does it hurt a lot?"

"Not too bad. It is a flesh wound. I just can't understand why the Palace guard acted that way. It is against the rules to threaten like that."

"How do you know?"

"Let's just say I know and leave it at that."

His terse tone makes me turn back to concentrating on my driving and leave him to suffer in silence. I wonder how he knows? I glance at him briefly. He has his eyes closed. I don't think he can die from a bullet wound to the arm. Can he?

Is there something in his past that I haven't been told? Nah. He doesn't look like anything but a camera man to me.

CHAPTER TWELVE

I hurry to see my Chief as soon as I get back to the office.

"Harry, you are not going to believe what just happened to us!" I say breathlessly as I sit in the chair opposite his desk. "After speaking to the Princess we were tailed and shot at! Stuart is in hospital with a flesh wound to his shoulder!"

"Yes I believe it. I got a call from the Palace. You are to be placed under restrictions and taken off any reporting on future Royal occasions," he says, smiling happily. "What did you do?"

"I only asked the Princess a few questions on how she got along with her father, what her real name is and if she really had to do all the work around the house," I reply, shaking my head in confusion. What is he so happy about? This is serious.

"I really can't see what the problem is. Why is there such a fuss over some questions?"

He starts to chuckle, a reaction I definitely didn't expect. He should be cross at me for upsetting the Royal family like this.

"You don't see what the problem is? Sylvia, you are a genius at acting dense! You are on the edge of breaking down a story that has never been challenged before. The fact they came after you and Stuart as a warning means you really upset the apple cart."

I hate to tell him I have no idea what he is talking about. I really can't see what I've done to the local fruit market.

"What should I do now though? I loved reporting on the Royal balls."

"Sylvia dear, I want you do to what you know you have to do."

I sit for a moment then stand up to leave.

"I have to make up the list of questions and present them to the lawyers."

"Good. Be the reporter you are and not just a pretty face in front of the camera," he says waving his hand to shoo me out of the room.

"Get on to it straight away. She invited you to present them so get it done. As soon as Stuart is cleared from the hospital, take him with you and deliver the list to Finlay's. I don't want you to go anywhere on your own."

I nod in agreement as I make my way to my desk.

I don't know what good Stuart will be but I don't want to go anywhere on my own with armed gunmen out on the loose. I am really impressed by Stuart and the way he handled the car so well, driving like a champion even when bumped from behind and his shoulder bleeding like it was. I might have flipped it over if I had been driving. Stuart remained calm through the whole thing. If he hadn't I doubt I would have been able to drive to the hospital and not panic.

Whew! What a morning! Now I have to think. That means a stiff drink of caffeine mixed with water.

I make my way through the maze of cubicles with high backs and computer screens. The glory days of the combined media centre are long gone.

All the other reporters are out trying to find something to sell to the television conglomerates or newspapers moguls. It is like fishing with any kind of bait you can think of to convince someone to say something they really shouldn't.

I finally reach my desk. The walls of my cubicle are covered with numerous photos of the many royal occasions I have been to over the years.

I really am a Royal supporter. Why would they treat me like this? Why would the Palace guards shoot at us?

As I look at the pictures and stories pinned on the walls I sigh with sadness. In each one my hair looks like it needs a good brushing and I have a stupid grin on my face. I have been a pretty face in front of the camera for so long I have almost forgotten how to do real research.

That is going to change right now! Quickly and before I can change my mind I reach out and start removing all the pictures of myself with various celebrities and signed photos of pop stars.

Finally I have reached the last one. I hesitate as I remove the first story I had printed in the Daily News before I turned to television. It was of the Royal Wedding and I was only seventeen, just out of school, wide eyed and full of dreams.

If what I have discovered is true, there is a lot more behind this story than meets the eye. Putting it all in the second drawer of my desk, I look around and smile, satisfied it is clear for the new phase of my reporting career.

I am now going to be an investigative reporter.

I sit at my cleared desk space, take out my notepad and look through the questions and answers I recorded from Charlotte Johansson Baker.

The body language of the two interviewees couldn't have been more different.

I had simply followed the story line and she had answered each question calmly and confidently even though she knew I had come with a preconceived idea of what she was like. The only one she hesitated over was out of line any way.

The Princess was guarded from the start. She had felt each question was an attack on her reputation.

How odd! Why would she feel like that? The only reason I can see for that is if what Charlotte has said is true and the Princess knows it.

In my heart I still can't accept that, though.

How could our precious Princess have been a spoiled, delinquent scheming in her pursuit of our Prince?

Charlotte hadn't said that, but it is something I picked up. It makes sense that in order for her to be able to afford a maid to do all the work she had to marry the Prince. What a lazy sod!

Pulling myself back to the present, I tap my pencil on the notepad.

I need to work out what the questions should be and how to ask them to see if this is the case.

They have to be worded in such a way they need to be elaborated on. Hmmmm.

How did she get along with her stepsisters? No, I decide to cross that one off the list. Of course she will say she didn't get along as she had to do the work and they got spoiled. Let's try another one.

How did she get her Debutante dress?

Yes, that should be a good one. I need to find a picture of the girls in their dresses so I can compare them. If she never got anything nice from her stepmother, then how did she get the dress?

I was actually surprised to hear she had gone to the yearly Debutante ball. Surely someone would have seen her there and reported the Cinderella story of neglect wasn't truthful. Mind you, who would believe them if they did?

Has she ever tried or succeeded in shoplifting?

Hmm. I wonder how she will react to this one. I can always relate the story Charlotte told me if she challenges it. I probably should ask Gabriella and Antoinette their sides of the story as well. If she says *no*, then that is final. Her word against her stepmother's.

Where did she get the dress?

Following straight after the shoplifting question, she will know what I am referring to. Yes, I will ask her that one. It makes more sense she stole it than for a Fairy Godmother with a magic wand to give it to her. I mean, if there really is a Fairy Godmother than why doesn't she come do my dishes when I beg her? Hmm?

Answer that one if you can, Princess. Oops, I am starting to get a bit cross now as I contemplate the possibility the public has been lied to for so long. I have to give her a chance to reply and not be so easily swayed from my support of her.

Why did you have to sleep in the tower?

I had forgotten to ask Charlotte about why Ella moved into the tower instead of staying in her own bedroom after getting so upset by the shoplifting allegation.

Maybe I should ask the Princess and pretend I know the true story behind it.

After all I must be a good actress for the Chief to think I actually know what I am doing.

My final question is the hardest. I have to make it expose the truth that may have been hidden with the other ones. Either way, this is the question most people want to know the truth behind.

When did she know she loved the Prince? When did she decide she wanted to marry him?

If she says she loved him from the party, then the story is true. If she says she loved him from a small girl, then maybe what Charlotte says is right. I need to ask Charlotte her view as well. I combine the two parts and smile with satisfaction. Done!

As I look through the list of questions I am surprised by the doubt I have in my mind. Have I started to believe Charlotte and not the Princess?

Maybe I'm still upset by the car 'accident' and Stuart being shot. The 'warning' has backfired on them if they think it will make me back off. I need to know the answers and so does the public.

Satisfied, I bring the list to the Chief to check through.

He holds his hand out without looking up, reads through the list carefully then chuckles.

"You are playing with fire," he says, leaning back in his chair looking at me over his wire rimmed glasses.

"Why?" I ask innocently. I know exactly what it looks like.

"Sylvia, stop playing dense. You have a list of questions here that will get to the very core of what went on. If you get truthful answers and explanations to any of these you will destroy a favorite fairy tale."

"I don't really want to destroy it!" I mumble. "I just want the truth to be known."

"What is the Truth?" he asks, holding the list out for me to take back. "The Truth is only discovered after both sides are heard and you find there is yet another side to it. A good investigative journalist follows every lead and lets the evidence reveal the truth."

I take the list and head for the door.

"I will pick Stuart up and go to the lawyers. The hospital called and said they have finished observing him and the bleeding has stopped. He needed a couple of stitches but it is nothing too serious. It was just a flesh wound."

"Good. Have him take the list to the lawyers. Remember you are supposed to be on restrictions," he laughs heartily.

"As if the Royals can control the media like that! They need to be put in their place and you are just the girl to do it."

"But I love the Royals!" I insist but my heart is not in the statement as much as it used to be.

"Yes, so do I but I love the Truth even more. That is why we are in this business."

"Okay," I sigh.

As I head for the car, I feel like I have stepped out of Fairy tale land and into the real world. What am I going to find next? Where will the answers to these questions lead me?

Chapter Thirteen

Stuart is dosed up on pain killers and his arm is in a sling so I have to drive.

The work car we normally use is in the body shop so I get to choose another one of the company cars. I look around and pick out a sturdy black four wheel drive the rural reporter normally uses.

If the Palace hoons come after us again, we won't be quite so easy to push around. I just hope they don't try again. I might not keep as controlled as Stuart did. I could cause a lot of damage if this chariot ran away with me.

Finlay Lawyers is in a fancy modern building in the centre of town. Before we can even get to the office we have to pass through a metal detector and place our thumb prints on a screen. Armed guards stand next to the elevators and watch us closely as we press the number for the fourth floor.

My nerves are playing havoc with me as I look around.

The guards are dressed similarly to the ones that attacked us. I hope we are not walking into a trap.

The elevator opens to a beautiful pink marble reception desk. We step out onto plush plum coloured carpet and past another armed guard.

What is it with all these guards? I have never noticed so many in my whole life. Have they always been around and I just never noticed them as I sailed blissfully through life? Have I really taken on this air-headed personae to such an extent that I don't see these things? Has my love of the royals blinded me to this? Or is there something much more sinister happening here?

The reporter in me is itching to write down and record everything I see.

The receptionist is waiting for one of us to say something.

Stuart walks up to the desk and hands her the list of questions.

"I am sorry but we don't have an appointment. We interviewed the Princess earlier today and she suggested we give her lawyer a list of the questions we want to ask. This is the list."

The receptionist is a strict, sour faced lady. Her grey hair is pulled up in a tight bun, giving her an odd kind of face lift. I can see her playing the role of a wicked stepmother quite easily. How ironic is that!

"Wait here please," she says, as she gets up and takes the list to one of the back offices.

She returns before we have had a chance to look around. That was super fast.

"You are to see Mr Finlay. Please go through."

I glance at Stuart in surprise. He raises his eyebrows in an unspoken question of 'what is going on?' I shrug my shoulders as we follow her.

How would I know? My brain is screaming *run* to my feet but the guards look too scary to carry it out.

Trying to walk as confidently as possible, we are led to Mr Cedric Finlay who is sitting at his desk.

He is short and round, a bit like the Fat Controller of a kids train story. His balding head is framed by huge thick rimmed glasses. He stands up to greet us as we walk into the room.

"Welcome Ms Stark and Mr Fitzgerald. I have been expecting you."

Puzzled, Stuart and I look at each other then back at him. Did we miss something in the Princess's invitation?

"We didn't have an appointment," I reply. "How could you expect us?"

"The Princess called to tell me she had invited you to leave a list of questions," he says, making himself comfortable in his seat.

We are sitting opposite him but not near as comfortably. The chairs have really straight backs and the cushions are as hard as rocks. Either they are designed to keep people from getting too comfortable and then staying too long or they are not used very often.

Either way, I am keen to keep moving.

"Oh, fair enough. We have brought the questions in. We thought we would just drop them off and leave," Stuart says. "Is there anything else we need to discuss?"

Cedric holds up the list and makes a show of reading it.

"No but I want to make sure I understand the context of each question before I give them to her Highness. The context will determine the depth and direction of her answers."

As he reads, his face turns redder with each one. I hope he is not going to have a heart attack!

What is so wrong with these questions? When he reaches the last one, he puts the sheet down, removes his glasses and rubs his eyes.

"I hope you realise these questions could lead to charges of defamation."

"What?!" I protest. Stuart kicks my foot but I move it away and take a deep breath before continuing much more controlled. "I am sorry, sir, but I don't see that. I haven't defamed the Princess!"

"Not against you, Ms Stark, but against Charlotte Johansson Baker," he says with a smirk.

Doesn't he think I realised that? All I am doing is asking the questions so how could I be defaming? Suddenly my serious reporter side kicks in. I am not going to sit here and let him think I am a dumb blonde bimbo.

"Mr Finlay, I must ask you to explain yourself. How can questions be defamatory? They are designed to draw out the *truth* of what happened in the Princess' past."

"I can see the motive behind the questions very clearly, Ms Stark."

"What you are really asking is whether or not the Princess has told the truth over all these years. If you find she hasn't been completely honest in every aspect then her reputation is destroyed. The image of perfection for each and every young girl is then tarnished. What can they aspire to then? Why aren't you trying to destroy Superman? Maybe he was on steroids? No one can get abs like that without chemical assistance."

"I understand your concerns but isn't the *truth* more important than an *image*?" I reply firmly.

"Not if that image is the Princess," he retorts. "If people find she is not the perfection of moral cleanness, grace and elegance, then who do they look up to?"

"Maybe setting a more realistic image is the way to go. Take her off her pedestal and make her *real!*" I insist. "It hurts a young girl's self esteem when she is never going to be as beautiful or elegant as this image."

"I can see you are determined to tarnish our Princess' image with your preconceived answers to these questions," he says, standing up. "You may leave now. I will put these to her Highness and we will be in touch."

"Thank you," I say as Stuart and I stand up and head for the door.

I know I was supposed to stay silent and let him do the talking but..... I can't. I don't have that kind of self control.

As we walk past the reception desk the secretary calls out. "Wait a moment please. I am just printing out the invoice for your visit."

Stunned I turn around, leaving Stuart standing next to the elevator door. "We just dropped off the questions."

"No, you went in to the office and spent time speaking with Mr Finlay." She insists, handing me a sheet of paper. "You took up his time so you pay for it."

As Stuart and I step into the elevator I look at the invoice in my hand.

Three hundred dollars for a fifteen minute minimum consultation. Now I know why there are so many armed guards around.

The lawyers are robbing the people and they are here to make sure we don't escape or react inappropriately.

I should have listened to my instinct and run when I had the chance. The Chief is going to kill us for this.

Chapter Fourteen

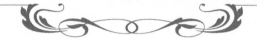

Back in the office, Stuart and I head to see the Chief first. $300 for 15 minutes? I am still shocked by the daylight robbery.

"What is this? I didn't approve a visit with the most expensive lawyers in town!" Harry protests when he sees the invoice. "I thought all you had to do was drop the sheet off?"

"It was!" Stuart replies. "Mr Finlay insisted on speaking to us to make sure he understood the context of each question before he puts the list to the Princess."

"He didn't even ask us about the questions, though." I add. "He just threatened to sue Charlotte for defamation."

"Sue for Defamation over questions?" Harry asks. "What is with that? What about just telling the truth!"

"Apparently if the Princess answers the questions truthfully it might tarnish her reputation thereby destroying the image of perfection for every girl," Stuart answers.

I glance at him, a little annoyed he is not being the silent partner he is supposed to be. I was supposed to be silent at the lawyers and didn't but that doesn't give him the right to take over now! When I see pain shoot across his face and his arm in a sling, I decide to let him speak as much as he wants. It is not just an interview for him. It has become personal from the instant the bullet entered his flesh.

Harry is watching Stuart as well and he must come to the same conclusion as he takes a stamp and slams it across the invoice.

"I'll pay this but I want you to find out what is really going on. For them to be so worried about her reputation she must have a lot to hide."

Nodding in agreement, we stand up to leave before he continues. "I want you to go back to Charlotte and get as much information as you can."

"If she is willing to speak to us," I reply. "If they have warned us off, I am sure they won't be leaving her alone."

Back at my desk I look through my copy of the questions again. What is so wrong with them?

"I have an appointment with Charlotte for two days time!" Stuart shouts across the room. "That gives us plenty of time to do some research."

"Us?" I ask as I come to his desk. "I thought you were just a camera man?"

"No, I was a reporter before I took up the camera. I found I lost the zeal needed to pursue a news story so I decided on a change. This is the first story I have felt enough passion for to want to sink my teeth into and it took a bullet to do that."

Well, I'll be! No wonder he keeps correcting me.

As we drive up to Charlotte's house I am amazed at the different feel I have about it this time. Yes, it is still very large, modern, and expensive looking but there is no pretense about it. Good on her if she had other investments to support herself in her older age.

The butler shows us into the same sitting room and brings some tea and scones.

Charlotte comes in, dressed in a grey pants suit, looking very professional with her hair in a soft bun. She doesn't have the sour faced 'wicked stepmother' look of the lawyer's receptionist but I can see a touch of sadness in her eyes.

"I just got back from a meeting with Mr Finlay," she says as she accepts a cup of tea from the butler and smiles her thanks. "I gather you met him a few days ago. Was that why you wanted this appointment with me?"

"Yes, he said a few things that worried us," I reply, watching her carefully.

I wonder what he wanted to speak to her about?

"Well, your list of questions sure stirred up a hornet's nest, my dear." She chuckles. "I must say I am impressed with them. You obviously believe what I told you which I am pleased to know. It is the inconvenient truth about Ella."

"What did he call you in for?" Stuart asks.

He is sitting next to me as we decided to have an informal meeting, off camera.

"Here," she says as she hands him a sheet of paper.

I lean over to look at it and gasp in shock. It is a Court Summons. The charges are for defamatory comments made regarding the Royal Princess.

"I am so sorry, Charlotte," I whisper, shaking my head. I can't believe it! He is carrying out his threat!

"Don't be, Sylvia. I am rather pleased actually. I will finally get my day in court," she says reassuringly. "Finally the battle between Stepmother and Stepdaughter can be handled publicly and legally."

I glance at Stuart. What have we caused? Suddenly I know what I have to do.

"I want to be there with you all the way."

Charlotte raises her eyebrows as she asks, "Aren't you under restrictions? You are not allowed to cover Royal events. Mr Finlay told me that today."

"Our Chief doesn't believe in political involvement in issues of public importance," Stuart replies. "However, if we are there to give you support, they really don't have a say."

"If that is what you want to do, then I am delighted to have your support," Charlotte says thoughtfully. "As long as you are aware your careers in this town may be over afterwards."

"Hopefully it will not come to that!" I say with more confidence than I feel. "Once the truth is out there, then surely people will see we were justified in pursuing it."

Charlotte looks at us both thoughtfully and then nods her head slowly.

"Well, I guess I had better tell you the whole story then."

CHAPTER FIFTEEN

The day of the court appearance approaches rapidly.

There has been a media frenzy during the last few weeks leading up to this time. The whole town seems to have turned out as the streets are filled with support for both sides. Banners line the sidewalk declaring 'Justice for Stepmothers' as well as 'Death to Dictators'.

I wonder who the Dictator is they are referring to?

The court room is filled with lawyers, media and guards.

Stuart and I sit next to Charlotte and her lawyer Sharon Stone. Sharon is an elderly lady who fits the role as a legal counsellor really well. In fact I would not be surprised if she got up and walked up to the Judge and said "Move over. That is my seat."

When the Princess arrives, a hush falls over the crowd.

She is dressed in a beautiful sky blue gown and long white gloves, looking just like the picture perfect princess she is portrayed to be.

Actually, now I come to think of it, hasn't she been wearing a sky blue gown every time I have seen her lately? What is with that?

Are the Palace maids insisting she put her own clothes away and since she refuses this is all she has left? I chuckle to myself, putting my hand over my mouth to keep anyone from seeing me.

How very disrespectful to laugh at the Princess! I'd probably get a fine or something if anyone saw me.

When everyone is seated Judge McKinley hammers his gavel on the desk. He is a tall, well-built man with grey hair who reminds me of my own father.

There is something about his face that makes me feel we are going to have a just decision made.

"The court is now in session and proceedings are about to begin," he announces. "First there is a reading of the charges."

The Clerk of the Court stands up and clears his voice.

"Uh Uh Um. The Royal Princess Cinderella is charging her stepmother Charlotte Johansson Baker with defamation, your Honour."

"Is that all?" the Judge asks incredulously, looking around the packed room.

"Yes, your Honour."

"On what grounds?"

"On the grounds of a list of questions submitted by the ABC reporters Sylvia Stark and Stuart Fitzgerald formulated from an interview with Mrs Johansson Baker, your Honour."

"So nothing was actually said?" the Judge asks, clearly confused like the rest of us.

"There are no two witnesses? No words spoken so a legal definition of defamation can be issued?"

"No, your Honour."

"Let me see this list of questions," he holds out his hand and the clerk places a sheet of paper in it.

While looking through the list, he glances over his glasses at Charlotte and then at Ella.

The court is restless as it waits for him to say something. Is he going to throw it out of the Court? I mean, really, there is no grounds for the charges. So what is all the fuss about?

After what seems like hours he finally leans forward and speaks straight into the microphone.

"After considering the fact no defamation has actually taken place, this court is clearly a waste of everyone's time and money. However I am curious as to the answers to these questions myself. Since testimony in a courtroom is not to be viewed as defamation as it is given under oath, I hereby dismiss the charges of defamation but impose the rights of the public to know the truth. A further hearing is in order."

Charlotte, Stuart and I sigh with relief. It is exactly what we had hoped for.

The lawyers on the side of the Princess start calling 'Objection, Your Honour, Objection!'

The Media in the gallery all start to shout out as well.

The Judge hammers his gavel to quiet the noise.

"I will give each side one week to get their witnesses together. We will meet back here and get to the bottom of this fairy tale once and for all."

With that he stands up and leaves the room.

The media frenzy hurries out of the building to report to the various offices. I see Freda, my Royal replacement, as she gives a little wave as she hurries out. I wish I could be reporting on this case but not only am I restricted from contacting any Royals but I have chosen a much more grand and noble position.

I am the media person for the Wicked Stepmother. I can do this as I am not reporting on a Royal event. What a great loop hole!

Charlotte, Stuart and I head out the back door to avoid the crowds. As soon as she is safe I will go out the front to give the media what they want. Information!

Just as we reach the back door a guard steps in front of us blocking our way. Charlotte stands with her head held high as she looks around and smiles.

Ella is sweeping her way towards us.

"How dare you?" she whispers angrily.

"How dare I what?" Charlotte asks firmly.

"I know what you are doing but it won't work. I will destroy you." Ella growls as she walks past and out the door, closely followed by her guards.

"Was that a threat here in the courthouse?" I ask, raising my eyebrows in surprise. "It sure sounded like it to me."

"Welcome to my world," Charlotte sighs. "You had better go feed the sharks, Sylvia. My butler can make sure I arrive home safely."

Stuart stands to one side while I climb to the top steps looking over the crowds. The media groupies are only just starting to work out what is happening. The crowd of ordinary citizens will have to wait until the evening news to know.

Suddenly I am bombarded by questions from all angles.

"What is in the list of questions?"

"Why didn't the Judge just throw it out?"

"Is there any truth to the defamation charges?"

"Whoa!" I say loudly, putting my hands up to block a microphone being shoved in my face. It manages to bump my nose before I push it away.

"One question at a time, *please!* If you want to know what is in the list, you will need to come here to court. I am not allowed to reveal any information on that."

"The Judge did throw the defamation case out but he retained the people involved. He obviously feels it is important to get the answers to these questions. There is no truth to the defamation charges against Charlotte but she may consider filing for just compensation against the Princess before this case is through. Ultimately the case will expose the truthfulness of the Cinderella story."

This causes an uproar from the crowds. How could anyone dare to charge their beautiful Princess?! She is perfect and poised! *Hah*! She is also very cunning.

"We will see you back here next week," I say as I push my way down the steps with Stuart as my bodyguard.

I feel like a bit of a celebrity as the reporters and camera men crowd around me, asking if a particular subject is on the list.

Is this what I look like when I am trying to interview someone? Pathetic and desperate?

Maybe this is what Charlotte meant about our careers being over in this town. It is only day one and I already feel sorry for the buzzards.

Chapter Sixteen

Stuart and I are back at Charlotte's house ready to discuss the next course of action.

"I am just going to tell the truth!" she says firmly. "I want to take the stand and finally have my say. It is time to stand up for myself."

"I wonder if there is a group of stepmothers out there who need to know what is going on? Surely you are not the only one going through this. You can stand up for all of them. What a great campaign strategy!" I quickly make a note on my pad.

"As soon as I get back to the office I'll arrange a few seconds on camera to contact others."

"I have never been very good at handling the media, Sylvia dear," she says softly. "I have to leave that in your capable hands."

"Great!" I reply, standing up excitedly. "I need to get back to the office and get this out on the air as soon as possible."

In the morning, as soon as I get in Harry calls me into his office.

"Sit down, Sylvia," he orders.

Oh No! What have I done now? I hope I'm not in trouble. Surely I can't be restricted to stay away from the court room just because the Royals are there. As soon as I sit down he bursts out laughing.

"What have you started? The phone is running hot."

It takes me a moment to work out what he is talking about.

"I only did a few seconds appeal to other stepmothers out there who have had difficult step daughters to come forward. We want to form the Stepmother's support group."

"You have enough support to start the Stepmother's army!" he chortles, passing several sheets of paper over the desk to me.

On it are the names and phone numbers of one hundred and fifty stepmothers who want to meet with Charlotte and myself.

"Oh!" is all I can think to say as I look down the list. This is a much bigger problem than I thought it would be.

"I have had a request from the Judge to subpoena your notes from the interview with Charlotte as it is what you would have used to base your list of questions on. They want the originals. I recommend you take a number of copies before you hand them over."

"Yes, sir." I stand up, still stunned by the support from the appeal.

"Sylvia, make sure you are never alone. Be careful," he warns.

The rest of the day is spent calling each woman on the list and arranging for a meeting to take place in the CWA hall.

Of course, each woman had to tell me her own tragic tale of injustice and hurt she had to suffer at the hands of her stepchild.

By the end of the day, I feel like making another appeal for fathers to reconsider remarrying at all, until their children have left home. No matter how hard these women tried they couldn't succeed.

Maybe I need to appeal for any successful stories next time. I can see this could really get out of hand quickly.

Imagine a whole new magazine being published on articles to help step families.

There are plenty of articles to help young girls dream of being Cinderellas. What about other groups? Surely they need somewhere to turn to for encouragement and ideas.

It is the day before the next court hearing and all the stepmothers are gathering in the hall. As they go inside, I hand them each a piece of paper. Finally it is time.

"Ladies, can I have some quiet please? Please find a seat," I say into the microphone.

It takes a few minutes for them to all find their seats and sit silently. Oh the power of a microphone. I love it.

"Thank you for supporting Charlotte by your presence here. As you know, being a stepmother is a thankless job. You fall in love with a man and have an instant family. The child may or may not live with you but one thing is sure, they resent the attention you are taking away from them."

I look around the audience and stop in surprise. There are a number of men here as well. Of course, men are stepparents too. They could have the same problems as the women. My magazine idea just jumped in potential readers.

"Of course, not all stepfamilies have these problems, but those who do, have nowhere to turn for support. Imagine if your family problems were distorted and then made into an international children's story? Movies are produced to highlight how bad you are? No one wants to know the truth as they prefer to believe the poor hard done by stepdaughter! After all, she is young and beautiful."

I can see the anguished look on the faces in front of me. Yep, they can imagine it alright.

"Well, the woman you are about to meet has had such an experience. Please welcome Charlotte Johansson Baker."

The crowd erupts in applause and stand up from their chairs as Charlotte comes to the stage. I can see the glimmer of tears in her eyes as she stands tall and well dressed in her grey pants suit. Her hair is loose, giving her a softer look. There is no trace of the typical Wicked Stepmother. She is clearly overwhelmed by the support she is getting from everyone in the room.

"Thank you," she whispers over the microphone.

A hush comes over the crowd.

"Thank you for being here. In case you are worried, there are no legal issues being faced here tonight as there are no charges. However, I will not reveal the list of questions my good friend Sylvia Stark has put together for the Judge to consider. If you saw them I am sure you would wonder what the fuss is over."

I can see the look of disappointment on quite a few faces. I had tried to explain to them on the phone this is not going to be a gossip session.

"The reason we wanted to get all of you together is to give me some kind of indication what the public think of the story of Cinderella. What part stands out to you? What part do you believe and what do you not believe? This will give my team the opportunity to go over the past and for me to do my best to remember. I am having a few senior moments, as you can imagine so the least surprises in court the better."

A wave of chuckling goes through the crowd.

Senior Moments quickly follow Baby Brain.

"Another thing I would like you to write down may take a bit more thinking. If the Princess was your stepdaughter and you were me, what would you ask her?"

Another wave of chuckling passes over the crowd and I just make out the word 'money'.

Charlotte must have heard it as well as she laughs and says "No, I will not ask her for money."

Her reply seems to set off a tidal wave of laughs and talking so she comes to sit next to me at the table to one side of the stage.

"You did very well," I whisper in her ear as I stand up to retake the stage.

"Ladies and the few Gentlemen in the audience. When you have finished writing down your suggestions, please make your way into the adjoining room where there are refreshments. You can get to know each other better then. Hopefully this meeting will also give you the chance to support each other and help you feel less alone in your struggles."

CHAPTER SEVENTEEN

The road to the courthouse is jammed packed with people. We have to work our way through the crowds to the front door, using the court guards to help.

I cannot understand why the Court lets us leave out the back but we have to arrive through the front.

It must be to feed the throngs. Or maybe it is to keep us away from the Royals.

From the top of the stairs, I pause and look around.

To my right is a group holding a large banner sign in front of them that says 'Step Parents Protesters'.

Signs saying things like 'Equal rights for Step Parents' and 'Say NO to Child Entitlement' can be seen throughout the group of over 200 men and women.

The group from last night must have come up with the idea. I smile as I tug on Charlotte's sleeve and point them out.

While she waves to her supporters I glance around the crowd further and stop stunned.

On my left is an equally large group of step children protesting with signs saying 'Stop Imitation Parents' and 'Stop Child Slavery'.

Stuart sees me looking at them and hurries me inside before I can go down the stairs and protest at their protest.

"The Princess has been busy getting her supporters together as well," he whispers in my ear. "Not so long ago you would have been the cheer leader for that side."

I jerk my head in surprise and start to argue when suddenly I realize what he said is true.

A flood of shame comes over me. Had I been so blind and narrow minded?

It takes a while for the court to come to attention with the media circus getting set up and then the Royal guards take their time checking everything in case a bomb has been planted.

Finally, Ella sweeps into the court room accompanied by the Prince.

A gasp comes from the lips of all the women in the court. He is sooo drop dead gorgeous! Now, *he* is male perfection. Superman has nothing on him! His black hair and blue green eyes are set off by the white, red and gold Royal uniform. I can feel my heart pounding faster than it should be when looking at a married man. Just having him present is going to make this case harder.

The Royal couple are so picture perfect it is hard to imagine they could be guilty of anything.

I shake my head sadly. I sure hope I haven't got Charlotte into water that is too deep for her to tread.

Finally Judge McKinley regains control of the court room.

"I request the two parties take their seats in the opposing witness booths," he says. "Any witnesses called will come to the box next to me."

As soon as they are in position, he continues. "There is no case to be proven here today other than to establish the truth of the Cinderella story. However, I must advise the Royal family, if the story is proven to be false, you may be ordered to pay compensation to Charlotte Johansson Baker. The amount will be decided by the Court in accordance to the amount of suffering that is determined."

A gasp can be heard in the crowd. I guess they never considered the possibility of that outcome. Why not? If I had been defamed on such a large scale, there is not enough money in the world that would recompense my suffering and ostracism.

"Let the court begin," the Judge announces as he picks up a sheet of paper. "Question One. How did you get your Debutante dress? Please will the Princess respond?"

I can see she is uncomfortable but since she is under oath, Ella maintains her poise and grace as she leans forward to answer the question.

"It was bought from the HD Ball Gown shop."

Charlotte's lawyer Sharon stands up and comes towards the booth.

"The story goes that you were neglected and only wore rags. Yet, here is a photo I want to submit to the court of the three girls at the ball. You will notice the dress is very nice indeed."

The Clerk takes the photo and passes it to the Judge.

Sharon continues. "According to the Ballgown shop, the dress you wore cost more than those of your stepsisters."

"Objection! Prejudicial!" Mr Finlay shouts.

"Overruled," the Judge says.

Mr Finlay looks around at the audience, clearly pretending he is in an important criminal case in some big city. Too bad there is no jury for him to play up to.

"When purchasing a garment for a member of a group, it is impossible to compare prices. One may not like the same style or they may already have a more expensive gown at home they plan to wear."

"Objection overruled. Please continue, Counsellor Stone."

"As I was saying, each of the garments were purchased on the same day and as we can see in the photo they were each worn to the same event. Can you please tell the court why you claimed you were deprived?"

Ella looks around elegantly using a tissue to wipe her brow.

"I had worked hard and the money spent on that garment was owed to me."

"Not according to the Cinderella story!" Sharon insists. "You were worked like a slave with no pay while the other girls got the nicer gowns. Here is evidence that was not the truth."

Mr Finlay stands up as he can see the Princess is struggling.

"There were no cameras in those days so how could a picture be taken?"

The Judge holds up the picture.

"It has been done by a formal portrait artist at the time. The signature is on the back."

Mr Finlay sits back down and Sharon returns to her seat.

"No more extra questions on Question one, your Honour."

Judge McKinley looks at the parties in front of him and shakes his head.

"It appears from the evidence, Question One has proven the inaccuracy of the Cinderella story."

"Excuse me Your Honour, but that is a bit of a big assumption to make over this one situation!" Mr Finlay objects.

"Is it?" the Judge asks. "Your client was not deprived of clothing and made to wear only rags as this picture clearly shows. Even if she had to wear rags at other times, that doesn't not prove neglect. My own children have more ragged play clothes and work clothes."

As the wind leaves Mr Finlay's sails, the Judge looks at the sheet again. "Question Two."

CHAPTER EIGHTEEN

"Why did you move into the Tower?" the Judge asks Ella. She sits silently, pale faced and by herself in the booth. "Please answer the question."

"My bed broke and my stepmother refused to fix it. The only other mattress was in the tower," she says trying to sound confident. "My ceiling leaked and it was horrible especially during winter. By moving to the tower I was closer to the kitchen where I could cook and clean and it was warmer."

I can hear a whisper of 'how cruel' echoing through the crowd.

The Judge sounds his gavel.

"Quiet in the court!" he shouts, scaring everyone with the suddenness of the loud noise.

Then he turns to Charlotte who has been sitting silently in the other booth.

"Ms Johansson, what is your view of this question? Why did Ella move into the tower?"

"Thank you for allowing me to respond, Your Honour. Ella had been grounded after sneaking out her window during the nights. I would often find her coming home in the morning smelling of alcohol."

"Objection!" Mr Finlay shouts. "Not relevant to the question!"

"Sustained," the Judge replies. "Please just answer the question, Ms Johansson."

"Very well. It was to keep her from sneaking out at nights."

Mr Finlay stands up and storms towards Charlotte's booth.

"What about her broken bed? Surely you didn't expect her to sleep in that?"

"No, sir. May I tell you why it was broken?"

"Of course," he sneers. "I guess you are going to say she was jumping on it?"

"No, sir. She had used the wood slats under the bed to form a ladder to help her get out of her window and to avoid the rose bush I planted there. Several of the slats broke."

A chuckle goes through the crowd. I guess they have tried it themselves.

"What about the leaking roof? Surely you do not expect a delicate child as the Princess was to endure such conditions?"

"Delicate child?" Charlotte tries not to laugh. "Mr Finlay, Ella is very skilled at climbing trees and making slingshots. She is not delicate. The hole in her ceiling was caused by one such slingshot during a particularly difficult temper tantrum. I had warned her numerous times not to shoot them inside but she refused to listen."

"Did she not have every reason to be angry? She was growing up with a wicked, controlling stepmother!" He protests.

Before Sharon has a chance to shout out an objection he says, "I retract that statement, Your Honour. Ms Johansson, why did you make her move into the Tower and not just fix the roof?"

"I didn't have the funds to keep repairing all the damage young Ella made out of her spite and frustration," Charlotte says softly.

"Yes, you did!" Ella calls out across the court room.

A collective gasp echoes through the room. Everyone is shocked by the outburst of the perfect princess. She seems to have shocked herself as she sinks into her seat and her face turns bright red.

Mr Finlay walks over to Ella and talks to her for a few minutes. I guess he is telling her to keep a lid on her emotions.

When he comes back, he is smiling wickedly.

"I would like to ask an additional question to Ms Johansson, Your Honour."

"Is it related to Question two?"

"It is related to my client's response."

"Go ahead. If I deem it is not relevant I will have it stricken."

"Thank you, Your Honour." Turning to Charlotte he asks "What happened to all the money from Mr Baker's Will?"

A gasp goes through the crowd as the Judge hammers his gavel. "That is not relevant."

Charlotte puts her hand up to speak.

"Excuse me, Your Honour. This is a core problem with this whole story. It is perceived I had money to spend on my children and not on her. If I may, I would like to answer Mr Finlay's question."

Judge McKinley smiles and nods in agreement.

"If you wish."

"There was no money, Mr Finlay. As I told the ABC reporter Sylvia Stark, Mr Baker had large medical bills left from his previous wife's illness. After his death I had to sell everything in the house to try to cover those bills. Even after that there was a lot more expenses left. I had a few investments

I had acquired before our marriage and Henry had signed a Pre-Nuptial agreement that I am happy to present to the court."

When she motions her hand, Sharon stands up and gives the documents to the Clerk who then passes them to the Judge. I smile to myself at this development. Having any documents on hand that supports her case is one of the suggestions made by the stepparents group.

"As you can see, I only received small payments each month from these investments and I was under no obligation what so ever to pay for Ella. However, due to my love for her father and for her, I chose to care for her as if she was one of my own."

Mr Finlay is standing in front of the Clerk with his mouth open in shock. Recovering a little he shakes his head.

"What happened to the money from the sale of the house?"

"I chose not to reimburse my investments if that is what you are wondering. That took place some years after Ella married and as you are fully aware, Mr Finlay, I gave the whole amount to Ella," Charlotte replies firmly.

"So as you can see, Your Honour, my children and I have suffered to provide for her, leaving us very little left over but I did not deliberately favour one over another."

The silence over the court room is so heavy I can hear a pen drop.

Judge McKinley clears his throat as he announces "Question three."

CHAPTER NINETEEN

"Have you ever tried or succeeded to shoplift?" the Judge asks looking over his glasses at me. "Ms Stark, how did you come about this question?"

"Please refer to the notes of my interview with Ms Johansson regarding the Debutante ball gown, Your Honour."

Silently he reads the notes and then looks up at the Princess.

"Please answer the question."

Ella shifts uncomfortably in her seat as she looks over at her husband. The Prince is watching her with amazement in his eyes. I am sure there is a lot he never knew about his perfect bride.

"Yes, Your Honour," she says softly.

A whisper of disbelief and shock goes through the crowd causing the Judge to hammer his gavel again.

"You tried or succeeded?" he asks.

"Both, Your Honour."

"Please explain your actions, Princess. Remember, you will not be charged but you may have to pay recompense for your actions."

"My stepsisters and I went shopping for the ball gowns and I picked out one I really loved. Of course my stepmother wanted me to wear a gown more suited to a child but I really wanted this particular one." She hesitates. "I tried to get my stepsister Gabriella to take it out of the shop for me but *she* stopped us."

The bitterness in her voice at the '*she*' can be clearly heard throughout the room. I am sure everyone else is just as disappointed and disillusioned as I felt when I first heard this. So far everything Charlotte had told me is accurate.

After all, what reason would she have to lie about what happened? She has already suffered for lies about things that didn't happen.

The Judge looks back at the notes and his eyes open wide when he sees the notes I made next to it. I smile and nod as he looks up at me.

Yep! Go ahead and ask the question!

"I am not sure if the second part of this question is related to Question four," he says, clearly unsettled by the connotations. "So I will ask them separately. Please explain the time you succeeded to shop lift."

I look around at the media personnel in the crowd. They are all riveted to what is unfolding. They are about to get some juicy gossip!

"I...I...I would like to take a break," the Princess says tearfully.

A guard rushes up to help her stand and leave the room. The Prince follows quickly behind her. Judge McKinley stares after them.

"I guess I had better call an intermission then. Be back in one hour."

The Clerk of the Court helps Charlotte out of the booth and invites us to go to the tea room behind the doors leading to the legal chambers.

"Thank you," Charlotte says as her butler hands her a cup of tea. "This is rather more traumatic than I thought it would be."

"I wonder how the next session will go. When the true story of no Fairy godmother comes out, oh boy, I hope there is no rioting," I say. "Imagine the publicity all this will get on the nightly news."

Just then the Clerk comes in to the room where we are relaxing.

"There is a riot outside the building. The court session has been cancelled due to safety concerns. You may want to go as quickly as possible."

"Will you accompany us to our car?" Stuart asks the Clerk. "We were threatened by the Princess when we left last time. I don't think Charlotte will be safe now there is a riot outside."

The Clerk nods. "I will get a couple of Court assigned guards to escort you home."

The crowds are surrounding the whole building, shouting and throwing cans and bottles. It is hard to tell which side they are on from the shouting and chaos.

As soon as Charlotte appears outside the back door a roar comes up from the crowd. They are obviously not on her side!

Shouts of death and revenge can be heard over the top of the barking police dogs and other voices shouting for control. The court guards hurry us into our vehicle.

Stuart jumps into the driver's seat and prepares to take off, just as an egg hits the windscreen.

His face loses all it's colour as he hits the deck, laying as flat as he can, nearly fitting completely under the steering wheel. Unfortunately he has already put the car into Drive and is now sitting on the accelerator so the car jumps forward and speeds straight into the crowds.

People dive out of the way and roll off the bonnet as a police siren and whistle sounds loud and clear nearby. Where is our escort?

Somehow I manage to steer from the passenger seat until we are out of the crowds and Stuart gets off the accelerator.

"That was a bit of excitement!" Charlotte laughs as she sits up from lying on the back seat. "I feel like a fugitive who has escaped from a watch house."

After taking a lot of detours and wrong turns, we finally arrive at Charlotte's house.

CHAPTER TWENTY

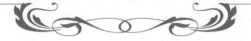

The next day I get a call from Charlotte before I even get out of bed.

"The court is going to be closed to the media today," she tells me. "I arrived early to avoid the madness. How soon can you get here?"

"I am Media," I remind her.

"No you aren't. You are my support team!" she chuckles. "I can't wait to hear Ella's response to Question four."

The street is a lot quieter today and we are way outnumbered by police presence inside and out.

As Judge McKinley takes his seat he indicates for the two parties to return to their booths.

"Let's get this over with, shall we?" he says. "I have had enough of the media circus. Today I want both parties to answer the questions as completely as possible with no ridiculous objections from their counsellors, okay?"

Everyone nods in agreement so the Court is declared in session.

"Princess Ella, please answer the question from yesterday. What did you succeed in shoplifting?"

Ella looks at the Judge and sighs. She appears resigned to the fact she has to answer these questions and nothing will prevent it.

"I stole the glass slippers, Your Honour."

I quickly turn to look at the Prince but he is hanging his head in shame. She must have told him yesterday.

"Please explain further."

"I had tried them on at the Ballgown shop. They were not meant to be worn, just on display by the mannequin. But they fit me perfectly."

"Why didn't you buy them?"

"I had no money and they were not for sale."

The Judge nods in understanding. I am not sure how he will handle this one. He looks at Sharon and Finlay.

"Anything further for Question Three?"

"No, Your Honour," they both reply.

"Okay, see that wasn't so hard!" He says, trying to smile. "Question Four. I thought this should have been included with Question One but you must have a reason, Ms Stark."

"Yes, Your Honour," I reply from my seat.

"Okay, Princess Ella, please answer the following question. How did you get the dress you wore to the ball?"

Ella gasps in surprise and looks over at the Prince and then at Mr Finlay. I wonder why the surprise? Surely she has gone through the list enough times. Maybe she thought it was removed?

"I am not sure how to answer that one, Your Honour," she says softly.

"Truthfully and completely would be good," he responds gently.

If the regular crowd was here I am sure a chuckle would have sounded through but instead it is completely quiet.

"Can I take a break?" she asks.

As a guard comes to her aid, Judge McKinley hammers his gavel.

"No! Stop procrastinating and answer the question. It should not be so hard!"

"You have no idea," she mumbles.

Finally she sighs and looks at the Judge, deliberately keeping from looking at the Prince.

"I was given it by a spy agency called Fairy Godmother's Incorporated," she explains. "I found them in the paper one day and sneaked out of the house to meet them. I was to go to the ball and leave an eavesdropping bug in the Palace. That was all I had to do and I could go to the ball in the dress of my choice. I was supposed to wait until after Charlotte and the sisters left, then they came and gave me the dress and quickly made up my hair. Next they dropped me off at the Palace."

The Judge tries to get his head around this. She had spoken so fast and soft he may not have heard it all but after a moment he nods.

"So... the Fairy Godmother did give you the dress," he chortles.

She looks surprised by his reaction.

"Yes, Your Honour."

"What happened when you went to leave?"

"I had to leave to return the dress before midnight so I rushed outside and they took the gown to return it to the shop. Instead of taking me home, they left me in the street so I had to walk home."

"So.... Let me get this straight. Your stepmother hadn't forbidden you to go?"

"No, sir."

"You wore stolen glass slippers?"

"Yes, sir."

"Why did you have to hurry like you did when you left? Obviously it had nothing to do with a midnight curfew and your carriage turning into a pumpkin."

"The shop keeper was there and she saw the slippers. I had already put the bug in place and I was enjoying dancing with the Prince. As soon as I saw her looking at my shoes I knew I had to leave quickly."

Judge McKinley sighs sadly as he looks at the few people in the audience of the closed court.

"I guess we have been fooled for many years. It almost doesn't seem worth asking the last question."

I look over at the Prince. His face is paler than normal and he looks like he wants to faint. I guess she didn't tell him about the spy agency until now. What a painful way to find out!

CHAPTER TWENTY ONE

Finally the time for the last question has come. The romantic in me wants to know this.

Surely it was love at first sight. The gorgeous girl and the handsome prince? Surely not all of the story is false.

Judge McKinley finally manages to compose himself.

"Okay, Question Five. Please answer this as truthfully and completely as possible," he reminds Ella.

"When did you fall in love with the Prince? Sorry, let me read the question as it is written. When did you first realise you were in love with and wanted to marry the Prince?"

Ella smiles softly as she looks towards her husband. Although he tries to smile in return, everyone watching can tell it is forced.

"I fell in love with him on the night of the Ball," she says softly. "When I first laid eyes on him."

"Objection!" Sharon calls out.

"What?!" the Judge protests. "How can you protest something like this?"

"Sir, I have here a diary Ella wrote while still living at home. It is a diary entry made just after her father died, six years before the ball in question."

Ella sits stunned and pale as she watches Sharon hand the diary to the Clerk who then passes it to the Judge.

Finlay comes up to have a look at it as well.

"Sustained," the Judge sighs. "Please continue Counsellor."

"The diary entry clearly states she intended to meet and marry the Prince as soon as she finished school. That was the only way she would be able to live the life she wanted."

"Yes, Counsellor, I can see that, but that is different to when she discovered she was in love with him."

"Yes, sir, but what it does show is Ella Baker is a cunning and scheming young woman who set out to trap our prince."

"Objection!" Finlay yells out.

I look over to see how the Prince is handling this. He doesn't look so good now.

"What is your objection?" the Judge asks. "The evidence does seem to indicate those attributes fit Ms Baker very well."

"She is Your Highness!" Finlay protests.

It seems a rather feeble excuse for an objection to me and the Judge has had enough as well.

"Okay, I will ask the question in two parts." He says as if all energy has been drained out of him. "When did you decide you wanted to marry the Prince?"

"As a young child I dreamed of being a princess just like all other girls my age," she admits.

"So when did you realise you loved him?"

"At the ball."

"Finally! Something is true about the Fairy tale!" the Judge says triumphantly.

A round of applause goes through the small crowd. What irony! Celebrating a single thread of truth in amongst a load of lies.

"Now that all the questions have been asked, are both parties satisfied the whole truth has been told?" Judge McKinley looks at the lawyers.

Sharon goes up to speak to Charlotte while Finlay goes to consult with the Royal couple.

"All is disclosed," Sharon says as she returns to her seat.

"Before you make a final ruling, I would like to put some questions to Charlotte if I may?" Mr Finlay asks. "The questions are relating to this case, Your Honour, and may alter your decision somewhat."

The Judge looks over where Charlotte is sitting leaning back in her chair, seemingly comfortable with the situation.

"Ms Johansson? Are you happy to take questions?"

"Your Honour, I would prefer the same dignity given to those on the opposite side of the room. If a list of questions can be provided, I will then be able to prepare a response to each one. Due to the hysteria we witnessed yesterday, a closed court is preferred."

"Fair enough," he nods in agreement. "Counsellor, prepare your questions and we will meet back here in one week's time."

CHAPTER TWENTY TWO

As soon as we can get out of the building and down the road, I turn back in my seat and look at Charlotte.

"What do you think the extra questions will be about?"

"I have no idea, my dear, but from what I have learnt in life, always expect the unexpected," she laughs. "I am keen to work my way through the questions and information supplied to us from the Stepmother's group. Maybe there is an angle I haven't thought about."

The days before the court case are more stressful than I had anticipated. For one thing, the questions don't arrive until half way through the week. When they do finally arrive, I am more puzzled than before. There are only three.

Where has Charlotte invested her money?

Has she ever heard of Fairy Godmother Inc. spy agency?

How did Charlotte get along with her daughters?

With the paper in front of me I call Charlotte for more information.

"How is this related to the Cinderella story?" I ask as soon as she answers the phone. "This has nothing to do with it."

"No it is not relevant at all," she admits. "I have just got off the phone from speaking to Judge McKinley and he agrees. The case is finished and he is considering compensation."

"What a relief!" I reply excitedly. "Do you feel vindicated?"

"Of course," she says. "I am sorry I don't sound as excited as I should be. I am really tired. I think the case has taken more out of me than I thought it would. I might go away somewhere for a while."

"That is a good idea. Make sure you leave a contact number with someone in case I need to get in touch with you."

As I hang up, I find myself smiling. The Cinderella story is debunked and I am happy about it. Go figure!

As I look through the questions from Mr Finlay a niggling idea comes creeping in. A good reporter always looks at both sides, unbiased by whatever the outcome will be. Maybe I should investigate these questions just as thoroughly as I did Charlotte's viewpoint.

To do this I will have to go visit Gabriella and Antoinette. Now I think about it, why weren't they here to support their mother?

I go into the office of my Chief deep in thought.

"What is wrong with you, sour puss?" he asks. "You should be celebrating. You have stood up for the underdog and exposed a whole network of need in the community. Stepmothers everywhere love you."

"I know but something is still bothering me. I am not being fair to the code of ethics a reporter is supposed to be."

"What do you mean? We have heard the one side of the daughter for years but you finally made us listen to the stepmother. You told both sides."

"Did I? Did I really? Or did I fall into the same trap as the ones telling the original story?"

"Go on. Explain yourself."

"Well, I feel there is something Charlotte and Ella are not telling us. I got a glimpse of it in the questions Mr Finlay sent for approval."

I hand the list to Harry so he can see what I mean.

"Why would Charlotte know about Fairy Godmothers? Why weren't Gabriella and Antoinette in court to support their mother? Charlotte managed to avoid saying where she got her money from, just admitting she got a small allowance from an investment to keep them going while the children grew up."

Harry hands the sheet back to me. There is no trace of the normal smile or joke on his face.

"I suggest you be very careful, Sylvia. If you find a deeper seed of corruption you may be facing not only the Royal household but also Charlotte. Remember the attack in the car?"

"How could I ever forget?"

"I know we assumed they were from the Royal family trying to keep you from getting the truth. But what if they are from someone else? Stuart said they were dressed like Palace special guards but anyone could disguise themselves like one. Why, I could hire one of those outfits from the Party shop, hire a goon mobile and fake guns and do the same thing. I know the guns were not fake but you get the point."

"Uh Oh."

"Yeah. Uh Oh," he replies, a smile starting to crease his face again. "I will support you as best as I can and assign Stuart to work with you but be very cautious. Behind the glitter and gold could be a lot of rust and corruption."

I stand up to return to my desk. I am even more worried now the Chief is being poetic. How much more upside down can the world get?

"Okay, I guess I had better get started then. Where do you suggest I start?"

"I suggest you go visit the two daughters to get their side of the story. Then find out how to contact Fairy Godmother's. Hopefully by then you will have some indication of what is going on."

Returning to my desk, I look at the questions again.

Yes, I have gotten Charlotte's viewpoint and also Ella's but not the two girls. Time to put that right.

Chapter Twenty Three

It is a drive of about an hour to the town of Flanagan where Gabriella Farmer is living. She has married the only doctor in the town and is living in one of the nicest houses. The house is a beautiful red brick home with a cottage style garden out the front. I can see a large vegetable garden out the back so she must be a hard worker to keep everything nice and neat as it is.

"Please come in, Ms Stark" she says, opening the door and ushering us inside.

"Nice to meet you, Mr Fitzgerald. I love your interviews on television, Ms Stark. It is a shame the Royal interviews have been taken over by the other girl. She is not nearly as natural and enthusiastic as you are."

"Please, call me Sylvia".

Gabriella is tall and slim with reddish brown hair and freckles. She is wearing jeans and a work shirt. We have clearly brought her inside from working in her garden.

"I am not sure what I can help you with. As you know from the Cinderella story, I never got on with my stepsister."

"Actually, we have found a lot of the Cinderella story is fairy tale, untruths and outright lies," I say firmly.

She looks up and raises her eyebrows as she asks "Really? I am surprised."

"Why? Surely you knew the difference between the story and what really happened. You lived it!"

"Oh yes, it was very different from the story but I never thought the truth would be revealed," she says, pouring herself a cup of tea.

"Why?"

She sips from her cup before she answers.

"Sometimes the truth can be a bit too inconvenient."

"Maybe you could clarify that?" Stuart asks when he sees she is reluctant to continue. I mean, the cup of tea is nice but not so nice as to forget to speak to your visitors.

"Maybe you could tell me what version of the "truth" you have heard then I can tell you my part," she finally says, putting her empty cup on the table and pouring herself another one.

"We heard about you trying to shoplift a ball gown for Ella," I tell her. "How about we start with that?"

"That is true," she replies, holding her tea cup to her mouth. She is making no attempt to fill in any more details.

"I have some questions I need to go through. Maybe it will help the conversation flow a bit," I say after waiting for a few minutes. "How did you get along with your mother?"

"Great. She worked so hard for us. I always felt horrible by the way she was slandered by the story. She tried to treat us equally but Ella was very difficult."

"How did you get along with Ella?"

"Good," she pauses again.

After a few more minutes of uncomfortable silence I look at the list of questions again. I have to find something to loosen her tongue.

"What would your mother know about Fairy Godmothers' Inc. the spy agency who gave Ella her outfit for the ball?"

Gabriella jerks her head in surprise. "What do you mean?"

"Just what I said. What would she know about Fairy Godmothers?" I repeat. There is something here. Her body language is screaming she is guilty but why?

"I think you need to ask her that question. Now if you don't mind I have a lot of work to get done today."

Gabriella stands up abruptly and heads for the door.

Stuart and I sit in stunned silence in the car. What had just happened? Have we touched another raw nerve?

It takes a half an hour to reach the City of Soho, where Antoinette lives. She has become a 'cat lady' living in a high rise modern apartment.

When she comes to the door I am surprised she hasn't married. She has long black hair and gorgeous alabaster skin. She could easily be a rival in the Beauty stakes with our Princess.

"Please come in, Stella and Stuart," she says waving her hand to show us the way to the lounge. "I am having a drink of scotch. Can I get you one?"

"Yes please!" I say enthusiastically. There is nothing better to loosen tongues than a nip of spirits. "On the rocks."

Stuart looks sad as he shakes his head. He is driving and still on pain killers from the gunshot wound. Painkillers and alcohol do not mix too well.

I have to be conscious not to sigh happily when the beautiful warming effect of the alcohol reaches my nerves and calms them down.

"A girl after my own heart," she says laughing musically.

I feel almost mesmerized by her movements. She is graceful and casual at the same time.

Sitting in the comfortable lounges and resting our feet on large cushions, the feeling of this place is completely different from others we have been to. Maybe we will be able to get some real answers here.

"We want to ask you some questions about your mother," I say, taking another sip of my drink. Whoa! This is nice! I have to keep control of *my* tongue if I have much more of this.

"Fire away," she says curling her feet up on her chair.

By the time we leave Netty's apartment, my mind is swirling. Besides the effects of two large nips of scotch, a completely different scenario is flashing in front of my eyes.

How come I never suspected it? Now I know about it the whole thing seems so obvious.

"What do you want to do now?" Stuart asks as he steers the car back to our office building

"I feel like having a sleep," I say with a slight slur. The scotch on an empty stomach wasn't such a good idea after all.

"In the morning I will call Charlotte to ask her for an explanation."

"I am sure you will get one but it may not be what you expect."

"No, I imagine it won't be. I still can't believe she *is* the Fairy Godmother and she was using all the girls as spies."

Chapter Twenty Four

For the next few days I try repeatedly to call Charlotte at her home but there is no reply. Finally I decide to drive over to her house. Stuart comes along but this time I insist on driving. I am cross! Why did she mislead us?

Knocking on the large door, I stand ready to ask her so many questions I can only hope they come out straight.

Finally, a maid comes to the door.

"I'm sorry, Ma'am and Sir," she says giving a slight curtsy, "My Lady has gone away on a short break."

"When will she be back?" I ask impatiently. "She said she would leave a number for me to contact her on if I needed to. Is there any way to get in touch with her?"

"I'm not certain. It is not my place to ask My Lady such questions," she says shyly. "I can only say that she took enough clothes to be away for a few weeks."

"Is the butler around? Maybe he knows," Stuart suggests.

"No, I'm sorry, he always goes with My Lady."

Frustrated we walk back to the car and sit there for a moment trying to work out what to do.

"Do you think Charlotte sent the thugs to warn us off talking to Ella?" I ask Stuart. "Harry thought there might be someone else involved."

He thinks for a moment.

"Possibly. It depends on what kind of spy agency she operates. She might have wanted to keep you from speaking to Ella because she knew if she upset the apple cart Ella would retaliate as she has."

I nod thoughtfully, ignoring the reference to the fruit shop.

"She would have hoped it would scare us away. It must have annoyed her when the Judge decided to follow the questions through. I looked at the Prince's response to Ella's confession of leaving the eavesdropping bug but I never thought to watch Charlotte."

"What is your plan then?" Stuart asks as I park the car at the office, but make no effort to get out.

"I am not sure if she is hiding or really resting. I want to confront her, but I have no idea where she is."

"I do," Stuart says, causing me to jerk my head around in surprise. "She never sold the old house she raised the girls in. She gave Ella the market value and transferred it into her maiden name."

"That means she has a lot more money than she has let on."

"It sure does. I wonder what else she is hiding?"

"Let's go find out," I reply, turning the car's engine back on and reversing out of the car park.

It is only half an hour's drive to get to the old house in Soho Heights, just to the north of the city. If she is not there we haven't wasted too much time.

As soon as we pull off the main road and onto the long drive way it is obvious someone is home. I stop the car just before we go through the last gateway surrounding the house.

From here we can see what is going on but are still protected from view by tall, thick hedges.

There are servants working in the garden, weeding and planting and one is pushing a lawnmower. From the upstairs window a maid is flapping a rug, getting the dust out of it. The house is getting a good clean up.

"Are you sure she still has this place? There are a lot of servants here. A lot more than in her town house."

"Yes, according to the lands title search I did it is still in her name. Actually to be more correct, it is in the name of Johansson Enterprises of which she is the joint owner and director with a brother named Charles. It's strange she never mentioned she has a brother."

"What does Johansson Enterprises do?"

"I have no idea. The computer search didn't show anything."

"I guess we should go and find out." I sigh as I put the vehicle into gear and start down the final turn of the driveway. "I feel like I am about to find the real Wicked Stepmother."

CHAPTER TWENTY FIVE

The butler answers the door, showing no sign of surprise that it is us. I guess it was only a matter of time before we tracked them down. We had been regular visitors to the town house. I am still puzzled why she never told us she was coming here.

"I will get My Lady," he says very formally.

He allows us to enter before closing the door and leading us to a small drab room. There is nothing of the spaciousness of the town house here. The sparse furniture is boring and old looking. The colour scheme of grey, black and yellow gives the overall feeling of depression and poverty. She must not have renovated it at all since they lived here while Ella was young. Maybe that is what she is doing here now? Suddenly I feel guilty about tracking her down.

Even after all the time we have spent with her, the butler is 'the butler'. He still has no name. I wonder if he is actually a body guard or a spy recruiter? Has he got a weapon hidden in his tuxedo or is he deadly enough with his hands?

This is the first time I have actually taken a close look at him. He is tall, thin and fit. I am sure I can see muscled shoulders under the fitted uniform. The way his arm sits I guess it is safe to assume he doesn't have a weapon hidden anywhere.

Then I look at his hands. They are not as soft as I imagine a butler's hands should be. No, this man doesn't need extra weapons as his are permanently attached.

Charlotte is a little easier to read. She is shocked and disappointed when she comes into the room and finds it is us. We are still standing as an uncomfortable feeling has kept us from sitting down.

"What are you doing here?" she whispers. "I told you I was going away for a while."

"You said you would leave a phone number for us to contact you with if something came up," I say firmly. I can't believe how much she fooled me. "Something came up."

She looks around nervously. "Couldn't it wait until I get back?"

"The maid didn't know when you would be back. Besides I thought you said you sold this house."

"Yes, well, my parent's company bought it. Ella wanted the money so I had no choice."

She is still keeping her voice really low and not sitting down. Her body language is screaming *guilty* but I have no idea what she is up to.

"What did you find that couldn't wait?"

"I decided to look into Fairy Godmother's Inc. I am sure you can guess who I found as the director."

Her face drops from a nervous smile to shock as she stares at me. "Is that all?"

"What do you mean 'Is that all'?!" I exclaim. "You were using the girls as spies, getting juicy gossip on everyone in town and getting them to leave eavesdropping bugs in planter baskets."

"Yes, well, I didn't want to tell you that is where I get my information from. The ones I listened to came from two different categories. Mainly they were people who were very financially savvy. I listened to find which shares to buy and which to sell. It isn't a very safe way to get information I know but no one wanted to talk to a single mother with three children. They just said to invest in a bank that gives you zero interest but is 'safe'. I needed more return than a 'safe' investment would give me."

"Who else did you spy on? What makes up the other category?" I ask suspiciously.

"I might have listened to you for a time to find out what sort of person you are. I didn't want to tell you my story only to find you were a Palace Plant," she chuckles. "You really need singing lessons though, my dear."

I blush to the roots of my hair. I like to dance and sing like no one can hear or see me because as far as I am aware, no one *is* watching or listening.

"Who else?"

"I try to help lonely ladies who believe their husbands are straying or who believe they have found the love of their lives to know for sure," she says shrugging her shoulders.

"That is why it is called Fairy Godmother's. Everyone wants to ask their Fairy Godmother what is going on in their loved one's life."

"So you aren't doing anything illegal?"

Nervously she glances away and then back again.

"No dear, I am not doing anything illegal. Now if you don't mind I really need to get back to my work."

The drive back to town is made in silence until we are once again sitting in the car park of the office.

"So what Netty said is right," I whisper while gazing out the window.

"Now what?" Stuart asks.

"I guess there is nothing left to do. We exposed the story and all the loose ends have been investigated. We just have to wait for the handing down of the verdict by the Judge."

"Back to regular reporting again then," he sighs. "I have enjoyed the adrenaline rush. We still don't know who tried to kill us."

"I am not sure what I am going to do," I say thoughtfully. "Maybe I should start a magazine for stepfamilies."

Chapter Twenty Six

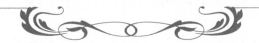

The next few days seem to drag.

I am glad I am not on the Royal reporting desk any more. I can't seem to get excited now I know what lies were told in regards to the Cinderella story.

I am not sure who to believe or to feel sorry for.

Without the emotion and passion it would be just reciting a he said/she said story.

The results of the last day in a closed court has been put under a media ban, preventing the release of any information.

I guess the Royals don't want their precious Princess to be exposed as the cunning, scheming vixen she is. I wonder who she was sneaking out of the house to meet. No wonder she got put in the tower. The public will never know the truth of the story.

I am a little disappointed but I can understand.

When the amount of compensation for suffering and injustice is revealed I am shocked and pleased. One million dollars for each year Charlotte cared for her after Henry's death. Two million dollars for each year of slander and one dollar per book ever sold, telling the fable of Cinderella.

That adds up to be ten million plus forty million plus one hundred million dollars. The total of One hundred and fifty million Dollars! What a gold mine! I guess anymore than that and the country would become bankrupt.

I wonder what Ella is going to have to do to repay the King all that money.

"I wonder what Charlotte will do with all that money!" I exclaim as I read the press release in the lunch room with Harry and Stuart. "Maybe we should go to the house and ask her?"

"Can't you leave the poor lady alone?" Harry says flapping the daily paper to get to another story. "The story is finished and the public are none the wiser."

"Poor? I don't think that word fits Charlotte Johansson Baker now." I laugh. "What do you think, Stuart? Shall we go have another interview to see how she is coping?"

"Why not?" he chuckles as he gets up from the table. "I will get the camera gear and meet you in the car."

The old house looks clean and fresh after its spring cleaning this last week.

I am impressed with the size of the old stone building. It must have been really hard to keep clean.

It is good to know the truth about the Baker family though. Ella had a normal upbringing even though she obviously wanted more. Don't all kids think they are hard done by at times?

It is hard enough for two parents to care for their own biological children without having one thrust on you from the age of ten.

The butler jerks in surprise when he opens the door to find us standing there.

"I am sorry," he says. "I don't believe My Lady expects any visitors today."

"I am sure she doesn't but could you let her know we are here?" I ask, smiling sweetly, ignoring his rudeness of not inviting us in.

I try to push past him but he firmly stands in the way and stares at me before closing the door, leaving us outside, as he goes to find Charlotte. Stuart and I look at each other in shock. What is going on here?

Finally Charlotte comes to the door and she is not happy at being disturbed. She is dressed in a silken house coat. Has she just got out of bed? Maybe she is sick? I hadn't thought of that.

Just as I start to apologise for getting her up she flares up angrily.

"What do you want now? Can't you leave me alone?"

"Whoa! Charlotte, I thought we were friends."

The sound of laughter and partying comes rushing down the hallway from the drawing room as the door opens slightly.

"*Mum!*" A familiar voice shouts. "You are missing the naked Twister game! It's your turn again."

Stuart and I stare past Charlotte as a beautiful slim blond woman dressed in tiny black lacy lingerie, fishnet stockings and garter belt comes part of the way out of the drawing room door, squeals then jumps back in, slamming the door behind her.

She obviously didn't know there were visitors at the front door but it isn't the way that she was dressed that surprises me the most.

It is Ella!

Before we can recover from the shock, Charlotte closes the door in front of us. The lock seems to echo in my head as it is turned. Clunk.

Or is that the penny that just dropped, putting all things into perspective.

As we drive back to the office I am still stunned into silence.

"Tell me what you are thinking," Stuart says as I pull the car into the office car park.

It is funny how this seems to be the place we do most of our best thinking. ·

"It has occurred to me that Ella is a year older than Antoinette who is one year older than Gabriella. When did Charlotte marry her first husband? Without birth control like we have today, she would have had Antoinette ten months later."

I pause to think this through before continuing to voice the images running through my head.

"Charlotte had said early in the first interview that a child born out of wedlock was given to a childless couple. I wonder if Henry had an affair with Charlotte? Were he and his wife Susan childless so Charlotte acted as a surrogate in the days when such a thing was condemned? If Charlotte ran the spy agency back then as I think she did, she would have known how much they wanted a child. Susan may have even employed her to check up on Henry. Could that be another reason why they married so quickly after Susan's death?"

Stuart nods his head in agreement.

"It is possible. In that case, if Ella is really Charlotte's daughter, she wasn't raised by her stepmother after all!"

"I have been meaning to ask you a question. How come you were supportive of Charlotte from the beginning?"

"I am the stepfather to a teenage girl," he laughs. "I know how sneaky they can be."

Suddenly I realise how little I know about my work partner. Maybe I should have asked his advice earlier.

We fall into silence for a bit longer as I think the scenario through. Of course silence for me is speaking my thoughts out loud.

"Charlotte admitted she used the girls to drop off eavesdropping bugs to listen for financial tips. If she was using the bug to find investment tips from the Palace, maybe later she decided there was a much more lucrative pot of gold to be attained?"

"The fact Ella fell in love with the Prince must have messed things up somewhat. Did they scheme together to get the compensation money from the Royal Family all along? Is that why she allowed herself to be slandered for so long, until she needed some money?"

"Possibly," Stuart replies.

"What about the Prince's search for Ella with the glass slipper? When he found her, why were Charlotte and the girls so angry? Was it jealousy as the story goes or was it because she would break up the nice little racket they had going?"

Stuart sits watching me as I think deeply on this. I sit silently as my thoughts keep skipping around so eventually he speaks up.

"I think you may be onto something."

"I can't help feeling there is something we haven't put out finger on yet. The pieces are all here."

I pause as I remember the scene we just left.

"Ella doesn't seem too upset with Charlotte by the way she is partying with her right now. Maybe she planned to get the compensation money to help provide for her mother and her sisters? After all, the way she called Charlotte 'Mum' she must know they are her half sisters, not step sisters. No matter how she was cared for, Charlotte clearly did her best under a very difficult situation. It must have cost her a lot."

Suddenly the pieces all fit together.

"That is it!" I exclaim. "No wonder no one ever challenged the Cinderella story. It was too convenient. It hid adultery, immorality, greed and deceit behind the façade of the Cinderella purity. The lowly downtrodden young maiden who suffers the injustice of others with grace, never getting angry, always beautiful and dignified, embodying the ideal values of good, piousness and ultimate virtue. It is what everyone wants to believe even though it is just a Fairy Tale. The true Cinderella doesn't exist! It was all a scam!"

A sense of relief floods over me quickly followed by despair. As the despair takes over, tears creep to my eyes. I have debunked the fairy tale in search of the Truth but now what?

Without Cinderella, who can girls look to for inspiration?

As soon as we get into the office Harry breaks the bad news.

The ratings have dipped drastically and I have to get back to fairy floss reporting.

No one cares about the truth if it doesn't make them feel good.

CHAPTER TWENTY SEVEN

"Welcome Viewers and Listeners! Sylvia Stark from ABC Celebrity News here with another exciting report outside the regular programming."

"It is often said there is a grain of truth behind each fairy tale we learned as a child. There is a moral to the story, a lesson to be learnt, a tale to be told, a love to share! Sigh. I do love reporting on romances."

"Anyway, as I was saying, somewhere in the beginning of time when the 'Once Upon a Time' was 'The Now' there was someone who lived the lesson, the moral, the love. We all know of stories like Cinderella, Snow White, and Little Red Riding Hood. But what about the ones that have not made the headlines as often? What about Humpty Dumpty?"

I pause as I wait for the invisible audience to consider the question.

"Yeah, I ask you what about equal rights for the short round people of this world? The ones not so beautiful and elegant as Cinderella? The clumsy and awkward need their voices heard too. Of course I know Humpty Dumpty is not a fairy tale but instead it is a nursery rhyme. Something totally different. So you may ask what am I talking about? Many people ask me that same question. Well, personally I think the saying still stands for Nursery Rhymes. There has to be a reason behind the story. After all why would we want to know about a cracked egg unless something is true about it and there is a lesson we all need to learn?"

Suddenly an image flashes in front of my eyes. Ugh! I hate it when an egg cracks before I get it over the bowl. *Yuck!* The feeling of the slimy stuff on my fingers! Forcing my brain to put that thought out of my mind for a moment until I can wash my hands, I plaster a smile on my face and return to the camera.

"There must be something in the story, right? Of course. I just hope it isn't about short, bald, fat people who are clumsy as this report would be pulled for being politically incorrect."

"Even if there is absolutely nothing true about it I just love the sing song way the rhyme always brings out of those reciting it."

"DAH dah DAH dah Dahdahdahdah. Don't you just love singing and the happy endorphins it produces! Don't you just love big words! In..door..fins! It makes me think of swimming indoors. It sounds so much more, I don't know, smart? Yes 'happy endorphin's' sounds so much more smart than 'happy feelings'. DAH dah DAH dah Dadadadah! I should have been a singer instead of a reporter. Sigh! *Ouch!*"

A small stone hits my shin, startling me back from my daydream. Stuart can see I am getting carried away as I put myself in the zone.

I actually hate this kind of reporting but I may as well have fun with it. Stuart knows. He feels the same. It has been six months since we exposed Cinderella and nothing has been the same since.

There was no truth behind that story and I haven't been able to find what lesson there was to be learned.

The feeling of betrayal still lies heavy on my shoulders.

I can't help getting carried away with this story. The ratings have shot up since our return to the regular spot but my frizzy blonde curls are not enough to keep the viewers and listeners enthralled anymore.

They want a real story. They loved the Cinderella expose but didn't care about the end. They always want more. Sigh!

I am still not allowed to report on Royal events but at least the listeners think I am funny, charming and enthralling. It is getting harder to make a good report while talking about Celebrity News. Most of the ones I have spoken to are gifted with good genes or lots of money before they became famous. I am blessed with my looks as well, but I really do feel sorry for those not so fortunate. People often think I am stupid, as I play the dumb blonde role so well, so I understand how unfair prejudice can be.

Oops, Stuart is playing with another stone. I'd better get back from my daydream and onto the story then.

"Oh sorry listeners and viewers. I tend to get carried away. Uh uh umm. As many of you may be aware, I have made it my personal mission to interview as many of the people behind these Fairy Tales and Nursery Rhymes as possible. I tried to get an appointment with Sleeping Beauty but she was resting. She must have Chronic Fatigue Syndrome, the poor girl."

A chuckle comes over the earpiece. *Yes!* Stuart likes that one.

"Today you are in for a special treat. I am outside the simple dwelling of Mr Harold Dumpt. It is believed the story of Humpty Dumpty came from him. I must ask him why he is called Humpty Dumpty? Make a note of that please, Stuart. Oh, you already have? Hehehe."

Stuart stands there behind the camera shaking his head at me. I wonder what he means? No? No what? I shrug my shoulders and force myself to concentrate.

"Before we go inside I really must refresh your memories of this cutesy little nursery rhyme. It is only a few lines but it tells a deep and meaningful story".

"At least I hope it does as that is what this whole report is about. I am sure you know it but I just can't resist the opportunity to sing. Stuart, do you have the music for this? What? No music? Sigh. Okay. Here goes. LaLaLaLa"

Humpty Dumpty sat on a wall.
Humpty Dumpty had a great fall.
All the king's horses and all the king's men
Couldn't put Humpty together again.

"Yes, Stuart, I know I wasn't supposed to sing it but it is a nursery rhyme! I am sure the listeners will appreciate the quality of my voice since I started singing lessons last week. I might even get a contract to produce an album once this goes to air!"

I press my hand against the earpiece so I can hear Stuart's mumble.

"That is not nice, Stuart. We need to get serious on this report!"

"So, over the last few weeks I have received numerous questions from you out there in Viewers Land, questions and observations you would like to put to Mr Dumpt. Now is the time to ask him what you really want to know. Some of those questions are:

Why was he sitting on the wall?

How long had he been sitting there?

Why did he fall off?

Did he fall asleep?"

"These are all intriguing questions and I am sure we will find the answers satisfying. I personally wonder how the horses got their hooves around the broken egg shells. I know how hard it is to walk on egg shells in my stilettos. I remember one time….."

A mumble comes over the earpiece again.

"Okay, I'll get on with the story. I must inform our young viewers they may be disappointed as this is not going to be a gory report where we walk through bloody body parts."

"Mr Dumpty isn't really a cracked egg splattered all over the ground. The poor egg is sometimes pictured laying there helplessly on the ground with his arms and legs and little vest scattered about…. Ugh! Stuart, that is gross! Why did you want me to say that? Oh, you didn't…. Make up your mind."

More mumbles come over the earpiece.

"Viewers and Listeners, my camera man just wanted you to know this is not a forensic interview. I apologise for getting your young ones so excited."

"Now, shall we continue? First for those listening I will tell you what I see around me while the camera spans the view for our television friends."

"The house is low set and made of white bricks on a very flat block with no fence in sight. I wonder if that is so he won't climb up and fall again? Hehehe. I want to crack up on that. Sorry, sick joke. Maybe I should be a comedian?"

Another mumble comes over the earpiece.

"*Don't You Dare* Stuart! I *am* trying!"

"Sorry, listeners. Back to the scene in front of me. There is no house on either side of Mr Dump's dwelling even though it is in a well built up area. I wonder why? Are they afraid of him climbing and falling over their fences?"

"What a walking public liability disaster it would be to have him living next door! HeHeHe. Uh Uh Um. I am having a really hard time concentrating on this story. Okay, a harder time than normal."

"Now, when I speak with Mr Dumpt I have been informed he doesn't like egg jokes. He is not cracked nor scrambled. HeHeHe. Apparently he is very mentally astute. I am only allowed to ask him questions related to the Nursery Rhyme. Since it is only four lines, this might be the shortest interview in the history of Celebrity News! ....I heard that!"

I walk closer to the house, giving Stuart a chance to fluff around rearranging cables and microphones. We really need to get a good juicy story so our Chief will give us the more modern equipment all the other reporters get. I am sure he doesn't view our work as important as other news so we have to make do with the old stuff. It is not fair!

Finally I am standing in front of the simple wooden door. I turn to smile at the camera.

"Are you ready? This is going to be such a treat! All this talking about eggs is making me hungry. I feel like having an omelette when I get home, Stuart. Okay! I hear you!"

"So viewers and listeners, can you hear I am knocking on the door? I like to knock three times. Knock, Knock, Knock. Three times for emphasis. Oh there is a door bell. Maybe I should press that as well. That reminds me of another song. LaLaLaLa *I'm going to knock on your door, ring on your bell, tap on your window too.*' HeHeHe."

Another mumble comes over the microphone. I turn to glare at Stuart. How dare he keep interrupting me! He makes it so hard to concentrate with his constant comments in my earpiece.

It is almost like I have another voice in my head, pushing my thoughts around. It must be getting very crowded in there.

"Oh! He is what? Here? Oh *here!*"

Quickly I turn and look at the man standing in front of me. In fact I can look him in the eyes in my stilettos which is very unusual for me. He has a bald head and is of rather sturdy build. Not fat or overweight, but he looks like he used to be extremely fit and now his muscles have lost their integrity over the years. I am surprise he is not more round and egg like as he is depicted. He actually looks rather distinguished with his bald head and grey eyebrows, almost like an old bald Tom Cruise.

At least I don't see any nose hairs! *Ugh!* Those things are gross! That is a major problem with being so short myself. I always have to look up to men when I interview them and see those hairs. It makes it so hard to concentrate seeing those things hanging out there like an alien trying to escape out of its body. When they are covered with snot it is even worse.

Oh he is still looking at me. Hehehe

"Hello, Mr Humpty Dumpty..... oh I am so sorry. I was distracted by your lack of heig... hair...Forget about that. Mr Dumpt, we are here for our appointment."

I brush my hair back with my left hand and congratulate myself on the cool save. I know how much people hate being told how short they are.

I have no idea why Stuart is smirking behind the camera.

CHAPTER TWENTY EIGHT

Mr Dumpt turns around and walks into the house so I follow, closely followed by Stuart as he makes sure the cable doesn't get tangled. I suppose I should try to make sure not to wave the handheld microphone around so much but I can't help looking around the house as we walk in. The house is immaculately tidy. In fact it is so tidy I am confused. Okay, more confused than normal. How can anyone live like this? Everything is perfectly in place.

We are shown to the lounge room and I take a seat opposite to where our host sits so Stuart can set up his camera. So far Mr Dumpt hasn't said anything. He is just staring at me as if I am an alien. I guess he hasn't seen so much hair in a long time. My hair seems to be standing out on its end as if to show off.

A short round gray haired lady comes in and sets tea cups in front of us as well as a small plate of store bought cookies. Most people bake cookies for our interview so I am a little disappointed. Maybe she ate them all. Now *she* could be described as egg shaped!

I chuckle to myself as an image of her rolling down a hill flashes into my mind. Stuart would be proud of me if he knew

I was controlling myself so well. She smiles at me then sits in the seat next to Mr Dumpt. I smile nervously as they sit there silently looking at me. I hadn't expected anyone else here. I wonder who she is?

"As I said when I made this appointment, Mr Dumpt, I have a number of questions I would like to ask you from our viewers and listeners."

"I understand, Ms Stark. I will answer anything that doesn't not put myself or my wife, Camilla, in any further risk." He nods and finally speaks in a deep voice with a strong accent.

I hadn't expected such a strong voice from a small man.

Is he Russian? German? Polish?

A picture of someone polishing his bald head flashes through my brain. *Stop it*. I tell myself.

The lady sitting next to him smiles. Ah! She must be his wife. Interesting. There is nothing known about Mr Dumpty and his personal life. Maybe I can get some gossip here.

Risk? What kind of danger could he be in?

"Thank you so much. I thought I would recite parts of the Nursery Rhyme and maybe you could explain what it was really about. How does that sound?"

He nods, still watching me and Stuart carefully.

He is sitting forward in his chair clearly not comfortable with the situation. Either that or he is in a lot of pain. I wonder just how cracked up he is? How many bones did he break when he fell?

Suddenly the image of him as an egg splattered on the ground flits into my brain. I gasp at the image then die of embarrassment as his eyebrows rise on the clear slate of his forehead.

They seem to travel further up than on a normal persons face, uninhibited due to the absence of a hairline. Can he read my mind?

"Sorry, I tend to get distracted sometimes," I mumble. I clear my voice and look at my note pad.

"The first question I wish to ask comes from one of our viewers. How did you get the name Humpty Dumpty?"

Although he still looks serious, a tinge of humour creases his face and the tension relaxes out of his body a little. Is he about to laugh?

"That is an interesting question," he says, finally forcing the sides of his mouth to rise in a smile.

"I have an unusual surname. At school I had to tell teachers how to spell it properly. D...U...M...P...T. I would say 'Dump with a T' so eventually they started to say Dumpty or Dumped. Of course since my first name is Harold it soon became either Harry, Hairless or Humpty."

He sighs as he shakes his head.

"Children can be so cruel."

"But you were an adult when the nursery rhyme was created. Why were you called Humpty Dumpty then? Was it a continuation of the childhood nickname?"

"I am not willing to answer that question," he says seriously.

His wife even sits up stiffly. I wonder what is really going on here?

"I...I...I am sorry?" I stammer as I look at them.

I glance at Stuart for support. He is frowning as well. This was definitely not the reaction we had thought we would get. I wonder what is the true story behind the rhyme?

My curiosity level is starting to climb.

"Okay, let's move along. The first line says 'Humpty Dumpty sat on a wall'. Did you like to climb walls?"

For the first time I do not feel like singing the verse. The tension in the room is still very high. Why did he agree to the interview if he is not willing to answer the questions?

He relaxes again and a smile starts to crease his face.

"Yes, I was always climbing things as a child. Trees, poles, buildings, fences and yes, walls."

"Did you often fall off? Did you break any bones?"

Finally a small chuckle comes from deep inside his throat. His wife even smiles and shakes her head.

"Never. I was the proverbial Spider man of the neighbourhood."

This time it is my turn to frown. That is definitely not the answer I expected. Where do I go from here?

"So, why had you climbed this particular wall?"

"I have never been sure which wall the rhyme is referring to. However, I find walls fascinating. They are solid and fixed in place, giving a feeling of security and stability. They tend to hold something in or keep something out. By climbing a wall I can see what is on the other side."

"You were not a thief, were you? Or a peeping tom?" I ask cautiously, not sure what kind of reaction I will get.

One of the viewers wanted that question asked, so I'll blame them. I sigh with relief as he shakes his head and smiles.

"No, I was never a thief and definitely not a peeping Tom." He glances at his wife and she smiles back at him.

She would probably roll on him if he dared confess to such a thing. He would be an egg pancake! Mmmmm. I am starting to get hungry again.

"So you sat on a wall so you could see what was on the other side?"

"Yes, Ms Stark. Very simple, really."

"The next part of the verse says you had a great fall. If you were so good at climbing did you really have a great fall? Or was it just a little slip?"

"Not off the wall."

Suddenly the tension rises again and the smiles disappear. What is going on here? I feel like I am in a washing machine, spinning from one emotion to another.

"So…. What did you fall off of? What was the great fall from?"

"I am not happy to answer that question however I will try to help you understand there are different types of falls." He says in a deep serious voice. I feel mesmerized by the intensity it holds.

"If the stock market falls, does it really fall from a literal height?"

"I don't understand the stock market but I think it is from a money value." I try to sound as intelligent as possible.

Hey, I am blonde and beautiful so why do I need to be brainy as well? Besides I am the one to ask the questions normally.

"Yes, it is a figurative falling. Maybe you will understand another illustration. If a high powered politician is found to be corrupt and on the 'take', he takes a fall. What kind of fall is that?"

"Umm…" I hesitate. A mumble comes over my earpiece. I must remember to thank the extra voice in my head later.

"He suffers a fall from Position, Power and Influence."

"Exactly."

The crease of a smile appears on his face as he starts to relax again.

"So are you saying you fell from your position?"

"I am not going to answer that, remember?"

The smile seems to be lasting longer this time.

– 133 –

"Oh, that's right. Sorry." I smile towards him then to the camera. This is a very strange interview. "So, you like to climb anything and you rarely ever fall but you had a fall that you didn't have off a wall. I guess that makes sense."

I look at my notepad again.

"My next question is about the King's horse and the King's men who couldn't put you together again. I have always wanted to ask you this. How can horses put anyone together? Wouldn't their hooves get in the way? I imagine it would be like trying to type on a computer keyboard with mittens on."

Finally a full chuckle comes out of his tense body.

"I am sorry for laughing, Ms Stark. The way you put that question is so funny." He chuckles. "I can understand the confusion though with the way it is worded in the rhyme. Maybe it is best for my wife to answer this question."

Camilla has been sitting quietly, rolling along through the waves of tension and humour we have had throughout the interview.

I expect a warm motherly voice but instead she speaks with a highly articulate professional sounding voice that is calm and deep. I am sure my surprise shows on my face but she remains completely composed as she explains.

"In ancient times a king's wealth and security was often dictated by the size of his army. The more horses and chariots he had the stronger and more successful the king is said to be. He could win more wars and plunder more loot. The referral to the king's horses in the Nursery Rhyme is actually referring to the wealth of the King."

I pause for a moment as I think about this explanation. Then turning to face Harold again, I ask the obvious question.

"So if that is the case, how come all the king's horses or his wealth, couldn't put you together again?"

A sudden chill runs through the room again. I expect the answer before he even replies.

"I am not willing to answer that question."

I look at Stuart who shrugs his shoulders. No help is coming from him.

"Okay, then, what about all the king's men? Is that referring to his influence?" I ask.

I am secretly proud I have made this connection when he nods. No extra voice in my head to help me this time.

"Precisely." Harold says, his smile coming back.

Are these two people bipolar when it comes to answering questions? Why do some get the cold treatment while others are okay? I can't see the difference but I will have to look into this further when I go over the recordings.

"So, that verse means the King's money and influence couldn't save you from the fall you didn't have off a wall?"

He looks at me with no emotion on his face at all then slowly shakes his head. He is not going to confirm nor deny anything no matter how I camouflage the question. Surely it is not as confusing for him as it is for me?

"The final part refers to putting you back together again. From the information you have given me, I gather it means you had a fall from your position or job and the king tried to get you off some charges but even his influence wasn't enough to restore you to your position. How scrambled up were you?"

I ask this question as I reason on what we have learned when suddenly it hits me! I have just done the unforgivable! I have made an egg joke!

He must be able to see the realisation come across my face as he stands up and heads towards the front door. For a man who is likened to a cracked egg, he sure is agile. Camilla stays sitting in her chair, her face closed off. There is no way this interview is going to be saved now.

"It is time for you to leave," he says firmly. "I realise now I should have never agreed to this interview without looking at the questions first. I heard what you did to the Princess."

As we walk out the door he whispers, "Be very careful. You already know too much. You need to watch your back."

I turn to ask him what he means but he closes the door leaving it only inches from my nose.

CHAPTER TWENTY NINE

Stuart and I are sitting in the car in the car park outside the ABC News office building.

"What did you make of that?" I ask him, leaning back in the car seat.

"I think Mr Dumpty is a rotten egg," he says.

Quickly I glance over at him to see his face covered with a full blown smirk. Finally we can use the egg references again.

"Is that why we always think of him as an egg? The rhyme doesn't actually say he is one but he is always pictured as it. I hate the way he is always cracked into dozens of pieces. His eyes are these beady little dots on part of the shell. I feel so sorry for him. I feel like crying when I read the picture story book to my niece and nephew. I go off eggs for a week afterwards."

Stuart thinks for a moment.

"I just said it as a funny comment but it does make sense if you reason on it further. He was definitely a hard boiled egg when you were trying to draw him out."

Ugh! Hard boiled. Rotten. EGGS! Hmmmm. Maybe there is something to this.

"An egg is made up of several parts. The white, the yolk and the hard outer shell covering. I wonder if there is anything symbolic about that?" I ask thoughtfully, not really expecting an answer.

Out of the corner of my eyes I can see Stuart jerk his head in surprise so I continue without turning to look at him.

"Yes, Stuart, I know what an egg is made of and I know what symbolic means. Just because I act like I'm dense doesn't mean I am."

His face still has the doubtful look on it but I am glad he doesn't say anything. I would hate to have to explain to my Chief why Stuart is in hospital with a broken nose. Besides I might break a finger nail.

"If it is symbolic, we need to find what each part means," he says softly.

I am secretly pleased he agrees with me so I feel compelled to continue.

"White normally means purity so maybe it is the good his work is supposed to achieve."

I don't even bother to look at Stuart but I can hear him gulp with surprise. I am determined to prove to him I am not stupid so I keep pursuing this train of thought.

"The yolk is more dense and is what the baby bird comes from. I hate to think of the number of baby birds that get killed every day just so we can have breakfast. However, back to the yolk. Things can hide in dense stuff. Maybe this is the true work he is doing. Do you think he is a spy working for the King?"

I turn to see Stuart is so impressed his mouth is hanging open. He uses his hand to put it back in place.

"It makes sense. The hard covering must then be the coat of legality it all hides behind. For some reason that cracked or exposed him to dangers that the King couldn't save him from."

"Yep," I say as I open the car door. "We need to get inside and work out our next move will be."

As we walk in the building the song runs through my head again.

Humpty Dumpty sat on a wall
Humpty Dumpty had a great fall
All the King's horses and all the King's men
Couldn't put Humpty together again.

For some reason I don't feel like singing this time.

My stomach sinks as I think of what we have found already. Is this the inconvenient truth about Harold Dumpt? Is he a disgraced spy?

The office is always busy, ever since the investigative report on Cinderella. Media outlets are clamoring for any gossip our freelance company can produce.

It took a while for Harry to allow me to select another story. I have been confined to simple and boring stories about pop stars and movie actors and even my questions have to be screened.

Finally I have been let free from the cage and allowed to select my own. Finally I can stretch my wings and let my imagination fly! I can soar to the heights in pursuit of the truth! Ugh. So many bird images remind me of cracked eggs again.

Of course Stuart is always by my side to make sure my imagination doesn't run too wild.

We never found out who it was who tried to kill us after asking the Princess a few questions. Stuart has this cute little scar he likes to show off whenever we have staff meetings to prove he has faced gunfire in the pursuit of a story.

The fact we were driving away as fast as possible and then hid behind some large containers is always overlooked.

A few heavily armed hoons said it was a warning against harassing the Princess. We would have responded to an email just as well.

"Do you think we might get another visit from the hoons?" Stuart asks as we walk to the office of Harry to let him know how the investigation is going.

"I hate it when you read my mind," I laugh but there is a real dampener on it. "Harold did say to be careful and watch our back. I don't understand it though."

"Watch your back?" Harry asks.

We have just opened his door. My, what good hearing he has. Another fairy tale springs to mind as I picture the Chief as the wolf in a red cloak waiting for Little Red Riding Hood. I shake my head to clear the scene. I have to concentrate.

"What have you done now, Sylvia? Please don't tell me you have already gotten into trouble on Day One off restrictions."

"It is not my fault," I protest. I try not to sound like I am having a whinge, but I hate it when I am unjustly accused of something. "Mr Dumpt is not what he appears to be."

"Just what does he appear to be that he doesn't appear to be then?" he asks leaning back in his chair. "Please spare me the cracked egg jokes."

Stuart fills him in on what we have discovered. As he tells it, I realise just how little we actually learned in the interview. We don't know what he fell off of. Neither do we know why the King's wealth and influence couldn't put him together again.

The only question he answered was his childhood nickname. Unfortunately Harry sees it the same way.

"So, you learned how the man got his nickname Humpty Dumpty. What else? *Nothing?!*" he asks clearly exasperated. "All the rest is hypothetical, supposition, and innuendos."

My, what big words he is using! For some reason I have always thought those three words meant roughly the same thing. I had better check my dictionary again.

"Yes, sir but it is what he didn't say that said the most," I reply. Stuart and Harry look at me with raised eyebrows. I must admit it does sound pretty dumb but it is true. "He refused to answer what he fell from, or what the King's men and horses tried to save him from."

"So, your point is?" Harry looks at me for a few minutes then sighs. "Okay, keep on to it then. Find out what he is hiding. I want a real story and not a fairy tale."

I am about to remind him Humpty Dumpty is a Nursery Rhyme and not a Fairy tale when I see Stuart shake his head.

Sighing deeply I turn around and head for my desk. I refuse to let him make me feel stupid. I make myself feel stupid enough without anyone else's help.

CHAPTER THIRTY

Sitting at my desk I look around for my pencil. It has to be here somewhere.

"Has someone taken my pencil?" I call out in frustration.

Oh where is it?! It is my favourite one I got from the Royal show last year and it has a little bell on the end of it.

The warning of Mr Dumpt has made me rather paranoid. I shake my head in frustration. I have to get something out of this.

I can hear a faint tingle of a bell as I shake my head so I do it again. Suddenly I put my hand to my hair where something is pressing against my head. Oh, it is my pencil lost in my frizz. HeHeHe. I must have tried to put it behind my ear at some stage. Nervously I look around to make sure no one saw me do that.

Sure enough, 'all seeing, all knowing' Stuart is watching, holding another pencil in his hand.

How sweet! He must have been going to give me another one. He shakes his head and looks back at his notes.

Casually I flatten down my hair trying to pretend nothing happened. I have to redeem myself with this story so I start to make a new list of questions around those he refused to answer.

First, What did he fall from?

Based on his explanation it could be a number of things. Was it influence, power or maybe his position as a spy was revealed? Why does the Nursery Rhyme say it was a wall? Hmmm.

I draw a picture of him sitting on a wall with a pair of binoculars. I can't help thinking he was a spy. I wonder if he still is? Oh how exciting it would be to expose an undercover operation of corruption! Since the King is involved, maybe it is foreign espionage?

As I remember what happened last time I got on the wrong side of the Royal family, I change my mind. Maybe that isn't such a good idea after all.

Hopefully Harold Dumpt is just an innocent man who really did fall from his position on a wall but it is too boring so he wants it to sound more exciting. I mean, whoever climbed as much as him without falling? Spiderman, pffft, sure!

Next, what had he done that was so bad the King and his influence couldn't put him back together again?

Again my mind returns to him as a spy. Did the foreign country he was spying on find out? What country was it? Will we have to go to war?

Oooh, I don't think I would look any good in front of the camera in army fatigues. Green and brown are not my colours. *Stop*! I force my brain to refocus.

The King is a good man. He has been ruling for a long time and everyone is happy with this. Surely he isn't using spies to watch other countries.

Maybe Mr Dumpt was a business man who fell sick in another country and the King had to get him extradited back home. Sigh. That doesn't fit either. I really cannot imagine what the real answer to this question could be other than him being a spy.

I wish there was some way to make him answer the questions. The tension in the room every time I asked certain questions may mean he is still afraid for some reason.

I wonder what would happen if the truth got out? If Mr Dumpt was a spy, what did he find that was so important the King had to step in to thwart a national disaster? Was Humpty Dumpty his code name? Was he spying over the wall when he fell?

If so, he may have been captured by enemy agents and tortured until he cracked. Hehehe, cracked! Get it?

My mind keeps going back to the one thing that makes any sense and I don't mean eggs.

Maybe I need to ask him what his line of employment was at the time? If he refuses to answer then what? I sit and think for a moment. Nothing comes to me. My head is empty of ideas. That is not unusual for me but this time it is disappointing. All I can think is, he is a spy.

"How do we nail a spy?" I ask Stuart as I make my way across the room to his desk.

"Do you think he is a spy?" he asks. "Why?"

"Because of what he didn't say. What do you think he is?"

"I don't know but we need to go to the Palace and ask the King a few questions."

I laugh at the idea.

"How on earth are we going to talk to the King? He never gives personal interviews!"

"No, but his publicity agent has agreed to give us a few minutes. If he thinks we have a case that needs to be answered by the King, maybe he will put the questions forward?"

"Ohhh!" I say excitedly, "An interview with the King!"

Quickly my mind races through all the things I need to get done before I do this interview. I need to get a new dress, a new hairdo and definitely a manicure. My heart is racing at the prospect of talking face to face with the King.

"No," Stuart, the wet blanket, reminds me. "An interview with his publicity agent."

"Okay," I sigh but I am still excited.

I haven't been allowed inside the Palace for a *long* time. After *that* interview with the Princess.

"Does he know it will be me doing the interview?"

"Yes, in fact he insisted on it," he replies, looking at me with a very serious expression.

A sinking feeling comes over me. Uh Oh.

Chapter Thirty One

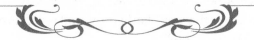

The drive up to the palace is just as beautiful as I remember it to be. The long sweeping driveway is lined with roses and across the green lawn in the distance I can see the tree lined river. A lake with white swans gracefully swimming amongst the perfect reflections of the trees lining the banks is so beautiful it reminds me of a puzzle I tried to do as a child.

As far as I am aware it is still sitting on my parents table waiting for me to return to put more than the outside pieces together. The reflections looked so much like the trees it became too hard to pick the right pieces.

Sometimes I think that reflects my life as well. It can be hard to know what is the public image I portray and who is the real me. The ditzy blonde is just a personae but at times.....Oh boy, that is a bit too deep. I can feel a headache coming on.

Two guards dressed in red and gold uniforms are standing at the entrance gate and they check our media identification before they allow us to go through.

Next to the front door are another two guards who walk up to us and point to an area off to one side. Stuart pulls the car in to the parking area then we get out and start removing the camera and gear.

"Cameras are not allowed inside the Palace!" One of the guards says firmly. "There is no recording of any interviews."

"But we have an interview with the King's Publicity agent, Mr Brown," I start to protest until Stuart puts his hand on my arm to stop me.

The guards have taken a step closer and look ready to kick us out. Oh my, what big guns they have. It is the first time I notice so I gulp as I stare at them.

"Okay, whatever you say. No need to get upset. We didn't know the rules have changed."

Stuart smiles at them as the guards take a step back to let us approach the front door. They don't seem to know how to smile in return.

What a stressful job they must have. We are only reporters but they seem to think we are a threat to national security.

Without the camera or microphone stuck in front of my face, I am really unsettled. At least I am allowed to bring along my note pad. Stuart is much more at ease than I am as he prepares to knock on the door.

The butler opens the door and looks startled to see it is us. It has been awhile since we have been here but we do have an appointment. He looks over his shoulder quickly and a guard comes up to stand next to him. Surely he is not scared of us? What does he think we will do? I have a note pad here loaded with questions, not a loaded gun. My questions are not dangerous…. Are they?

"We have an interview with Mr Brown." Stuart says, holding out a piece of paper he has taken from his coat pocket.

It is crumpled and looks very unprofessional but the butler passes it to the guard who carefully flattens it out and reads it then checks his watch.

"Yes, you are on time," the guard says softly and firmly. "I am to take you to the sitting room in the east wing."

Wow! Does that mean we get a tour of the Palace? I've never been to the East wing before. How exciting! I start to step over the threshold when suddenly I realise the guard has stepped right in front of me. He is coming outside!

A very slight smirk on his face shows he knows what I was thinking. Darn!

He leads us to the right side of the main entrance along a path that seems to head towards the back of the Palace.

Finally we arrive at an enclosed outdoor sitting area full of flowers and fernery. Swarms of beautiful butterflies are flitting among the leaves. We walk over a wooden bridge which crosses a small artificial stream. How peaceful!

Unfortunately the trickling of the water over the rocks is starting to play havoc with my bladder so unless I can use a royal bathroom I am going to have to keep this interview brief. Maybe that is the idea behind the location.

"Sit here!" the guard orders, pointing to a couple of chairs next to a table.

Sighing deep, I sit where I have been told. It is beautiful here but I had wanted to see inside the Palace again. Surely I am off restrictions here too. The guard goes through a sliding door into the main building, probably the East Wing, and returns a moment later with Mr Brown.

Mr Brown looks strangely familiar. He is tall with broad shoulders and dressed in a neat black suit. He has jet black hair and is wearing dark sunglasses. He doesn't look like a Publicity agent to me.

He looks more like a spy! Was he one of those who gave us the 'warning'?

Suddenly my nervous butterflies take flight to join the ones in the bushes. Along with them goes my confidence.

"Thank you for seeing us, Mr Brown," Stuart says, getting up to shake his hand. "I know you are busy so we will keep our questions brief."

"That is okay," he answers.

His voice is soft and warm. He would make a fantastic radio announcer. All the women would swoon every time he spoke.

"I understand you have some concerns about Mr Dumpt."

"Actually, we have some concerns about the Nursery Rhyme Humpty Dumpty," I say, interrupting Stuart before he can answer.

After all I am the interviewer! *And* he asked for me.

"We spoke to Mr Dumpt a couple of days ago, who as you are aware the rhyme is supposedly based on, and there were quite a few questions he was unwilling to answer."

"What makes you think I will be able to answer them if he won't?"

I look at Stuart, speechless. I hadn't thought about that. Coming here was Stuart's idea!

"We wanted to know what Mr Dumpt did while he was in your employ," Stuart says, referring to his own notepad. Humph! Give him a break and he takes over!

"You must be mistaken. I believe he has never been directly employed by the Royal household. Did he say he was in our employ?"

I jump in to reply.

"No but according to the Nursery Rhyme says the King's men and horses couldn't put him together again so he must be involved somehow. Was he contracted by the King to do something then?"

Mr Brown thinks for a moment.

"Yes, I believe you could say that."

"Then what was he contracted to do?"

"He was contracted to create masterpieces."

I sigh with frustration. This is as painful as pulling teeth. Each question is a struggle. I am glad Stuart is doing some of the interviewing as I might tell him to stop playing games and give us the information we want.

"What masterpieces was he employed to create?" Stuart asks calmly.

"Persistent aren't you?" Mr Brown says, chuckling softly.

The cutest dimple I have ever seen peeks out on his right cheek. A dimple and *that* voice! Sigh! I could fall in love with Mr Brown.

"It is nothing sinister as you obviously feel so I may as well tell you. Mr Dumpt is a tailor of the highest degree. He used to make the dresses and suits for the Royal family."

My mouth drops open in surprise. *What!?!?* Is that all! A dressmaker?!

"Why didn't he want to tell us that?" Stuart asks.

"Maybe you didn't ask him properly." Mr Brown shrugs his shoulders. "I know he is a very private man and the contract he signed stipulates the Royal Family members are not his walking billboards."

"Then according to the Nursery Rhyme, he had a great fall but if he is a dressmaker, what did he fall from?" I ask, keeping my voice as calm as Stuart's.

Stuart looks at me with raised eyebrows. What? Doesn't he think I can control my temper?

"For reasons I will not disclose, the Royal family decided not to use him any longer. Soon afterwards, I believe his business shut down or changed to produce other garments. Since he no longer carried the prestigious title of 'Royal Dressmaker' maybe that is the great fall being referred to? I really don't know."

"Why would the King want to use his wealth and influence to put him back together again? If he is just a dress maker, then why the fuss?"

My voice is starting to show the frustration I am feeling. I am not getting the answers I thought I would. A dress maker?! How boring!

"Ms Stark, I know you suspect the members of the Royal family of being dishonest. But they are still human and very empathetic when it comes to the welfare of businesses in the town. The King didn't want Mr Dumpt to lose his business so he tried to refer him to other wealthy individuals. Unfortunately, I understand it wasn't enough work to keep him making the beautiful gowns he was renowned for."

"I do not suspect the Royal family of being dishonest." I protest but Stuart puts his hand up to stop me from continuing.

Sighing deeply to regain my composure I continue.

"So the rhyme is really about a dressmaker who sat on a wall because he liked to climb. Then he lost his business due to the change in the Royal dress designs and taste."

How absurd!

Mr Brown nods his head in agreement as he stands up and offers to shake our hands.

"I can see you don't want to believe it but that is the inconvenient truth of the story as far as I am aware."

The guard leads us back over the bridge and to our car. Silently Stuart drives as I think of what was said. Something doesn't make sense.

"Here," Stuart says as he pulls a small tape recorder from his pocket. "See if there is anything we can use on this."

"You sneaky devil!" I laugh as I rewind the recorder then press play.

"*This recording has been blocked.....This recording has been blocked....*" is all that comes over the speaker.

Stuart looks at me, stunned.

"How did they know? They must have had a scrambler in the area and taped that over it."

Suddenly *thump*!

A hit from behind sends our car fishtailing out of control and across several lanes of traffic. Stuart fights with the steering wheel to regain control. I look behind and see a large black hummer on our tail.

Not again!!

Chapter Thirty Two

Stuart plants his foot heavily on the accelerator and the car leaps forward just in time to avoid another hit from the black hummer.

We are speeding and weaving wildly through the traffic as we try to keep out of reach of our pursuers.

Where are the police when you need them? If we were doing this to get somewhere I am sure we would have a dozen cars with pretty flashing lights following us.

"Get the license plate number!" Stuart shouts as he pulls heavily on the steering wheel to avoid a slower car.

How dare they do the speed limit in the fast lane!

I turn in my seat and look at the vehicle still racing after us.

"There is no plate!"

"Great!" He mumbles. "Hang on!"

He pulls heavily again to take the highway exit at the last minute and then up onto the footpath to keep from slamming in the back of cars stopped at a traffic light.

I look behind and sure enough the black hummer is still behind us.

"Where are we going?" I ask, hanging on and ducking down as our vehicle plows through several fruit stalls, sending apples and oranges flying through the air. We are really upsetting apple carts now!

This sort of thing always looks so much fun when watching it on a movie but in real life it is much more scary. I expect a watermelon to break the windscreen at any moment.

"Here," he says with a broad smile as he pulls into a compound surrounded with a high wire fence.

I look around frantically and there is no exit. All I can see is a lot of other cars and the high fence.

"*Oh no!* We are trapped!" I cry out.

He stops the car at the back of the building but my brain has gone into over drive. There is no protection here and nowhere to hide!

The hummer will be here any second. I am sure we are about to be shot at so I duck down as low in the seat as I can.

We are going to die! I am not ready to go yet! I want to get married and have children. Those things take more time than I have facing me right now. The killers will be here any minute!

"Calm down," he says with incredible control. "Look around."

Finally I manage to pull myself up from the floor to see where we are.

Stuart has pulled us into the vehicle compound of the Royal Valley Police Department. We are surrounded by police squad cars!

"Take some deep breaths," he says softly. "You are hyperventilating. Don't you dare faint on me!"

Taking deep breaths seems to clear my head. No, I am not going to die. No, the hummer didn't follow us in here.

Clever Stuart. I start laughing hysterically as relief sets in and Stuart joins me.

As I look out of the front of the car and see the police officers approaching, my laugh slowly runs dry. Why do they have their pistols drawn and pointed at us?

"Get out of the car with your hands up!" one of the officers yells.

His gun is pointing at Stuart. I glance at Stuart and his face is so white I doubt he will be able to stand up when he does get out.

"Come on, Stuart," I whisper as I squeeze his hand and peel it off the steering wheel.

"You can do this. We have to get out and explain what just happened. They must be worried that we are some idiots who have driven in here by mistake while trying to escape a bank robbery or something. We did make a rather fast and grand entrance. You did some pretty fancy driving. You could be a stunt car driver for a movie."

He looks at me and smiles as the colour slowly starts to return to his face. It is good to see. A bit of humour goes a long way. I just hope we can talk our way out of this without being arrested. We get out of the car at the same time.

"Get your hands up!" The officer yells so we obediently put our hands up at the same time.

Suddenly my brain snaps and I start to wiggle my heels left and right and wave my hands from side to side while keeping my arms up. My head bops up and down to an imagined beat. DAH dah DAH dah Dadadadah.

The beat of Humpty Dumpty is echoing around in my head taking my body on a trip of its own.

"Stop that!" The officer yells while trying to keep from laughing.

Stuart shakes his head, clearly embarrassed by my behavior. "She is Sylvia Stark. She can't help it."

"Oh! Put your hands down then." The officer smiles and lowers his gun. "I thought we had some genuine bad guys here, not a couple of nutty reporters."

Stuart and I lower our arms and my brain clicks back into reality. What had I just done? How embarrassing!

"I am sorry for the speed of our arrival," Stuart says. "We had a black hummer without a license plate on our tail. The last time that happened I got shot."

The look on the officer's face changes to one of shock and I can tell we won't get away from here for a while. I still need to use a toilet in a Royal hurry.

"Come in and tell us what just happened and about your previous experience," he says. "We can't have this sort of thing going on."

After a couple hours in the police interview room, I am more than ready to go home. My brain is so overloaded with events I can't think straight.

Finally Officer Smith decides we can leave. He opens the door at the back of the building to let us go the quick way back to our car and as I walk past he leans over and whispers.

"Be careful. Watch your back."

I turn to ask him what he means but he closes the door within an inch of my nose.

I hate it when people do that. What is it with all these warnings? I haven't done anything wrong.

Do they think I have eyes in the back of my head?

CHAPTER THIRTY THREE

Finally we are back at the office and reporting to Harry.

Stuart explains what happened and even includes my little impromptu performance.

I am sure my face is so red it is even changing the colour of my hair. How embarrassing!

Harry laughs.

"Genius! Sheer genius!! Sylvia, you never fail to amaze me! You broke the tension and probably saved your butts with that dance routine."

Genius? Me? That is one word that has never been used to describe me but I will take any compliments from my boss that I can get.

"Thank you, sir," I mutter.

"And you managed to get more information to clarify Harold Dumpt's relationship with the Royals as well," he says nodding in approval. "Mr Dumpt was the Royal dressmaker and he got Dumped. Do you get it? Dumpt got Dumped!"

He starts laughing again and Stuart joins him. I chuckle but I don't really feel it. I am very disappointed the nursery rhyme is such a fizzer. I had wanted something exciting.

"Why didn't he just say that? Why didn't he want to tell us he made the Royal gowns?"

"Maybe his lips are stitched! He is all sewn up legally!" Harry smiles and slowly gains control of his laughter as he sees I am serious.

I guess he finds sewing jokes funnier than those about eggs.

"Do you think there is still something in this?"

"Yes, I do. When I asked Mr Dumpt why he was called Humpty Dumpty as an adult he refused to answer. He could have said the name just stuck or that was the name of his shop, or whatever. I believe it is a code name for something else. Maybe he did more than make dresses. Maybe he was smuggling something in with the fabrics."

Stuart raises his eyebrows as he listens. Yes, Stuart, I am capable of putting pieces of a pattern together. Maybe not as well as a dress maker but......

"That's it!" I exclaim. "Pieces of a pattern."

I turn and rush to my desk to grab my notepad. When I return I can see they are puzzled.

"Can't you see? It has to do with the Cinderella story somehow. Mr Dumpt makes the dresses with hidden pockets. Ella and her sisters were spies, working for Fairy Godmothers spy agency, looking for unfaithful partners. She uses the dresses to drop the eavesdropping bugs she has hidden in the pockets!"

"So?" Stuart and Harry ask at the same time.

"The same black hummer attacks us after we go to the Palace."

"So?"

I sigh.

"So.... I don't know. I admit I can see the pieces but I have no idea how they fit together. I have never been any good at puzzles with more than 250 pieces."

Harry nods his head.

"Okay. You have had a busy day. Finish up and go home for a rest. Take the weekend off. By the time you come in on Monday, hopefully you will be able to see the next step clearly. You might have to leave this story and look for another one. I don't know of anyone who would care about the tale of a dressmaker who fell off a ladder or whatever."

I start to correct him but decide it is not worth the effort.

Being told to take the weekend off as a Celebrity reporter is almost like being told to stop breathing.

That is when all the events happen. All the scandal and intrigue, all the performances and ......maybe I do need to get another job.

Is that what the Chief really means? Have I lost my edge? I never had an edge but have I lost whatever it was that made me top of the ratings?

I pull my little red car into my garage and sit for a few minutes.

What is happening to me? Am I seeing things where there is nothing to be found?

I want to be a real investigative reporter but the story has to be there. I can't create it but nothing much happens here in our city.

A lot of fairy tales and nursery rhymes got their beginnings here but they are from a long time ago. That magical time of Once Upon a Time. I really should have been reporting then.

Sighing sadly I get out of the car and press the button to close the roller door. Suddenly a wave of extreme heat floods over me and everything turns black.

CHAPTER THIRTY FOUR

Before I open my eyes I can tell I am lying flat on an uncomfortable bed. It must be a hospital bed as I can hear the beeping of a machine nearby. Carefully I open my eyes and wiggle my fingers. Everything works but I feel a bit stiff. I wonder what happened?

"So Sleeping Beauty awakes."

The soft voice of Officer Smith whispers in my ear.

His smiling face fills my view as I try to move to see around me. He is a fairly old man, probably about ready to retire, with a grandfather's face, kind and open. His grey hair makes him look quite distinguished. I smile back at him and start to move around so I can sit up in bed. He puts his hand on my shoulder to keep me down.

"Don't move. You have a few burns that aren't ready to be moved yet."

Burns?

"What happened?" I ask even though my throat is really sore and dry.

"Someone planted a bomb in your carport. Your car protected you from the worse of it."

"Bomb?"

"Yes, Ms Stark. Someone wanted you dead or at least out of the way for a while."

Oh no! If they came after me I wonder if they went after Stuart as well?

"Where is Stuart?" I ask anxiously.

Suddenly I need to sit up. If someone wants me dead how do I know it is not Smith? Where is the one person I know I can trust? Where is Stuart?

"He is just outside the room getting something to eat. Whoever set the bomb must not have thought he was as much of a danger as you so they didn't go after him. He is okay."

"Why?"

My throat is really sore so I force my arm to move towards the cup on table. Officer Smith picks up the cup and arranges the straw so I can drink. It is so refreshing! Why would someone try to kill me?

"Why? That is one question I don't understand. Why target you?" Smith laughs.

Can I hear a bit of sarcasm in his tone of voice?

"I meant why attack us at all?" I say as firmly as I can.

A nurse comes in and helps me sit up. I feel much better now I can see around me.

My legs are wrapped in bandages and my arms look like they have had a major case of sunburn. I am dressed in an extra large floral nightgown, the kind I would give to my blind grandmother.

My hair feels crisp and frizzed out on the ends like a giant afro. Oh boy, what a photo opportunity! *Not!*

Officer Smith watches me as I look at the injuries.

"You got off very lightly. No major burns, nothing worse than severe sunburn on all your exposed skin as you can see.

What they call Flash Burns. If you had a longer skirt on you would have been better protected. You fainted straight away so your eyes are okay. Your car wasn't so lucky. You are going to need a new paint job at the very least."

The bandages go right up my thighs so I have to wiggle around a little to get comfortable. I can feel gel packs under the bandages to take the heat out of the burns. After the bandages come off I am going to need a swim in some skin lotion. I remember getting a sunburn while at the beach and it wasn't nice.

Ouch! This is going to be itchy!

Suddenly something occurs to me. What is Smith doing here next to my hospital bed? I had only met him earlier that day. I look at him and frown.

"What are you doing here? What is really going on?"

His head jerks back in surprise.

"Well, aren't you a quick one? Maybe I was wrong about you."

"That is not an answer. What is really going on?"

Smith nods and sighs deeply.

"Okay. I guess you should know since you came so close to being fried."

"Wait!" I tell him quickly, holding up my hand. "Wait until Stuart is here."

Finally Stuart comes into the room. I had started getting suspicious he wasn't really here since it had taken him so long. The hospital cafeteria must be a long way away and very busy.

The whole time Officer Smith has been watching everything I do. It is very nerve racking. What am I? His daily entertainment?

Doesn't he have something else to do? *Anything?*

"Now you can tell us what is really going on." I tell Officer Smith as soon as Stuart comes in and sits down.

He doesn't look very happy. I wonder what he has to be so upset about? I am the one feeling like a half fried mummy.

"We have suspected Mr Dumpt of being a spy for some time but we could never catch him saying anything suspicious. When you went to interview him we were listening over some eavesdropping bugs we have planted around his house. It was the most we have been able to get out of him for years. We really wanted to know what he fell from so when he refused to answer we decided to dig a bit deeper. Have you heard of Fairy Godmother's Incorporated?"

Carefully I nod my head as my heart sinks into my stomach. Yes, I have heard of Fairy Godmother's spy agency. Please tell me Humpty Dumpty is not related to the Cinderella story somehow! I had thought that when speaking to Harry earlier but deep down I really had hoped it wasn't so.

"Well, it appears he may have been employed by them to spy for their clients."

"But Mr Brown said Mr Dumpt was a dressmaker!" I protest.

I can see this is new for Officer Smith as he sits back and thinks for a moment.

"That is another thing I don't understand. After our chat at the police headquarters I checked up on this Mr Brown. There is no such person at the Palace."

I look at Stuart in surprise. He had been the one to make the appointment. Had he checked who we were actually going to be speaking to? Stuart is sitting a little behind Smith so when he shakes his head and puts his finger to his mouth he is out of Smith's sight.

"Then who did we speak to?" I ask, not sure what Stuart wants me to not talk about.

"That is something I want to find out. You didn't get a recording of the interview did you? I might be able to recognize his voice."

"No," Stuart says before I can tell him about the scrambled tape. "They made sure we didn't take anything to record or film with."

"Hmmm. That is too bad." Officer Smith says, leaning forward to make sure I am focussing on him and not Stuart. He must have noticed Stuart's interruption stopped me from saying something.

"Was there anything you can remember about him?"

Again Stuart starts to speak up. "No, I told....."

I can tell from the grumpy tone of Stuart's voice he wants me to keep quiet and not give anything away. Since I don't know anything, that is easy, so I shake my head.

"No. He looked just like any thug we might meet in the street. Black suit, average build and black hair and he wore sunglasses."

Officer Smith seems happy with the answers so he stand up to leave.

"Have a good rest. I will see you later."

As soon as he leaves Stuart moves to the seat closer to my bed. Holding my hand he looks around the room.

This personal contact with my work partner makes me uncomfortable so I take my hand out of his grip. We might joke around but personal space is always respected. Nothing has changed as far as I am concerned. Still, he looks really worried about something that he is hesitating to tell me.

"What?" I ask. "What is wrong?"

"Where do you think we are?"

"In the hospital in town."

He shakes his head cautiously, glancing towards the door and then leans over to whisper in my ear.

"No, we are in some kind of hide out. I think Officer Smith is with the Royal Secret Service and not on the good side."

"What?" I whisper back. "What do you mean?"

"We have been kidnapped."

CHAPTER THIRTY FIVE

Having a weekend off for a Celebrity reporter is like a death knell for their career, right? However, if you are being kept against your will by the Secret Service under the employ of the Royal Family then it can be a gold mine. At least that is the way I prefer to see it. Maybe I will be able to get some new equipment after all!

Stuart is free to come into my room where I am receiving medical attention for my burns whereas I have to stay put.

Luckily the burns are all superficial and only time is needed to heal them properly. Still it is so good to have the cooling effects of the lotions the nurse puts on them on a regular basis.

Without it I am sure I would scratch them and break open the blisters.

"There is no way out of here," Stuart whispers on the third day. "There is no one around except Officer Smith and the nurse."

After a few more days have passed, I am starting to get restless. The blisters are going down and I am tired of resting. As soon as Officer Smith comes to visit I need to know when I can leave. It must be almost the weekend again.

I am a Celebrity reporter who lives for the weekends.

"Smith, I want to go home," I insist.

"You are not well enough," he replies firmly.

"Then why can't Stuart leave and go home to his family? I know I am not in a hospital and that he is here to visit me, so don't try to give me that excuse anymore."

"We are keeping him here for his own safety."

"I don't believe that. You said the bombers went after me and not him," I say firmly. "I want to go home. The Chief will worry about where we are."

"The Chief? Who? Your boss, Harry Parker?" he laughs. "No, he thinks you are having a holiday. He told you to take some days off, didn't he?"

How does he know that? He must have slipped an eavesdropping bug in our pocket or somewhere to hear that. Is that why he timed this little abduction now? Now that I am over the shock and effects of the burns the seriousness of the situation is sinking in.

What is he waiting for? Who will rescue us?

If the Chief thinks we are on holiday then we are not being held for ransom. Smith hasn't said we are being kept here against our will so I decide to push the issue until he does. I want to find out *why* I am here.

"Why would he think that?" I ask. "He knows I am on a case and that I would never just walk away from it."

"Maybe he thinks you and Stuart have run away together," Smith laughs wickedly. "You are very close so it makes sense. You two are always flirting together and the chemistry is what makes your reports so entertaining."

The idea of being romantically involved with Stuart is so absurd I can't think of any comeback to it. He is obviously trying to distract me from asking the important question so I will ask it outright.

"Why have you kidnapped us?"

Suddenly he stops laughing. "Kidnap you? Is that what you think?"

"Yes, you refuse to let us leave and you have made up stories that are not true. Stop answering my questions with questions! It is so annoying."

"Aren't you two a romantic item?"

The serious look on his face tells me he hasn't thought it through.

"*No!*" I laugh even though I am annoyed he has done it again. "And stop answering with a question. He is married and we are purely co-workers. The closeness on camera is just a performance. Surely you have noticed we have not been all over each other since we have been here."

"Oh!" Quickly he stands up and hurries out of the room.

A few minutes later Stuart comes into my room with a big smile on his face. "Smith sure left in a hurry. What did you say this time?"

"He thought we were a romantic item."

"And you told him I was married?"

"Of course."

"Oh," he says sadly. "That explains it."

"What?"

"Smith didn't know about my wife so he has gone to find her. I hope she has managed to get away to safety by now."

I shake my head to clear it. "What is going on? It has been five days and no one will answer my logical questions."

"Sylvia, I believe we are being held by the ones who caused Mr Dumpt to have his big fall. They are out to get him for some reason and if they can use us to do that then they will."

"But why would he come for us?"

"I am not sure yet. The Prince told us Dumpt was a dressmaker, right?"

"Yes."

"You remember you said there was some kind of pattern?"

"Yes."

"I reckon Mr Dumpt is a code breaker. He looks for patterns and creates masterpieces meaning he is essential in national security."

"How did you find out this?"

"Officer Smith thinks we know more than we do. He asked me some very interesting questions. I used to work in security before starting with journalism so I could see where he was leading. He is not as good as you are though. He gives away a lot more than he realises. I just repeat what he has already told me."

Getting such a compliment from Stuart almost makes me lose track of what I need to know.

"Wait! You said the Prince talked to us. I thought it was Mr Brown his publicity agent."

"Smith found there is no such person as Brown. The man we spoke to was obviously in disguise but I recognised it was the Prince by the dimple on his cheek when he smiled. Of course I didn't let Smith know."

"You should have told me! You mean I spoke with the Prince and didn't even know it?" I ask while trying to keep my voice as low as possible.

What a useless Celebrity reporter I am!

"He wanted to be incognito but it must have been very important for him to speak to us."

I look at him for a moment.

"Stuart, answer me truthfully. How did you get that interview?"

"I used to be one of the Palace elite bodyguards. He owed me a favour."

I lay back on my bed and close my eyes. Surely I will wake up and discover all this is a bad dream. I interviewed the Prince of our wonderful country and didn't even recognise him! No one gets to interview the Prince unless he calls a generic press conference and even then the questions are all scrutinized and modified.

I could have asked him anything I wanted. How will I ever live this down?! Sighing deeply I push the depressing thought out of my head.

"So, whatever Mr Dumpt is up to must have been pretty serious stuff. But why did the Prince lie to us?"

"I don't know. I'm not sure he did lie to us. He is either a professional liar or he really believed what he was saying. His body language showed he was relaxed but also concerned."

We lapse into silence for a long time, each lost in our own thoughts. Is Dumpt a spy? Will he come rescue us? Why would he do that? What is really going on? Will my hair ever be right again?

"How are we going to get out of here?" I whisper.

"I have no idea," Stuart replies. "I just hope my wife has left town already."

"Why would she leave?" I open my eyes and sit back up.

"After the run in with the Hummer the first time I told her if I don't come home she is to leave town as fast as possible. She is also to call the Chief so he will know we are not off on a naughty trip. I figured that would be the most logical excuse someone would use. I called her just before I left the office to head home and told her it happened again and reminded her of the arrangement."

I look at him in awe. What a smart partner I have!

"That is so good. Stuart, you are amazing. Someone may be looking for us after all."

"I just wish there was some way of getting out of here. I have walked around everywhere I have been allowed to go but there is no obvious ways out. All the doors are locked except yours. My room is right next door."

"Do you know where we are? Are we still in town?"

"I think we are under the Police Department vehicle compound building," he replies, keeping his voice low and glancing around.

He must suspect there are listening devices to pick up any bits we let out. I hope they didn't catch the bit about the Prince. Too late to worry about that now.

"I was stopped on the way home and loaded into a black van. Before they took me out of the back they put a bag over my head but I could hear the highway nearby."

"I wonder if anyone will think to come looking for us here? We must have been here nearly a week."

All of a sudden the lights go out, plunging us into complete blackness.

Chapter Thirty Six

People are yelling and screaming in fear as the blackness swallows us. It feels like we are in the belly of a huge monster. I can't hear myself think nor even see my hand in front of my face.

"Will you stop screaming?" Stuart says sharply, right next to my ear.

As soon as I stop I realise I am the one doing all the screaming and the sound has echoed around the solid walls of the bunker. Just as well no one can see my face glowing red with embarrassment. All around is dense darkness and deathly silence. I wonder what time it is?

"Stand up," Stuart whispers, taking me by the hand. "There must be a storm outside. We have to get out of here before the lights come back on. Maybe the cut in the electricity will allow the doors to be unlocked manually."

"How do you know your way around?" I ask as we carefully make our way along the black corridors.

I can see some faint emergency night lights ahead, lighting the way. Duh! He had just finished saying he has looked around the whole area and checked every door. He must have memorised the pathway to any external doors.

As soon as we are in the corridor lined with the tiny lights we can move a lot faster but Stuart holds my hand so I do not get lost or crash into him. We stop every so often to check there is no one following us.

All around us is deathly silence but the echoing sounds of our footsteps sound like huge elephant thumps. Everyone must have gone home for the night. It may not even be night time but there are no windows to be able to tell.

Suddenly, Stuart stops and presses me against a wall with one arm as he listens. I can hear the sounds of fast approaching footsteps running along the corridor. We try to hide in a doorway, hoping the person will run straight past but just as he starts to pass us, I gasp in surprise.

It is Mr Dumpt, dressed completely in black. At least I think it is him. Whoever it is, is short and has a black balaclava over their head. Only his eyes are showing and even they are only slits. It is too dark to tell.

"You are the noisiest prisoners I have ever had to rescue," a voice grumbles in a deep muffled voice, coming to a stop next to us. "Come on. Follow me. And *please* keep quiet. The officers are looking around outside the building."

Suddenly he turns around and starts racing along the corridor and out the door at the end. Stuart drags me along with him. My arms and legs are still stiff and sore from the burns and bandages and being in bed for nearly a week.

I must look like a cross between a mummy and a hysterical witch by the way my hair has frizzed out. To make it worse I have to run stiff legged as if I have done something in my underpants. Stuart had better not tell anyone about this!

As we race out the door I see Mr Dumpt jump onto a wall and disappear over the other side.

Oh no! Humpty Dumpty sat on a wall, Humpty Dumpty had a great fall?!

I run to the wall and look over the other side, sighing with relief as there is no sign of him anywhere. How did he disappear like that?

"Let's get out of here," Stuart whispers as he runs up to me and grabs my hand again. "We are outside the compound."

I look around and sure enough he is right. We have come out through a trap door in the side of a ditch on the outside of the chain mesh vehicle compound.

Flashlights are flitting around like fireflies inside the compound while the officers on duty tonight are looking around for who knows what. I wonder what Harold used to distract them? Was this the same way I was brought in while I was unconscious?

"How are we going to get away?"

He holds up the keys to his car.

"I had the spare set in my pocket the whole time and I can see my car is parked in the compound. We are going to have to break in and steal it."

I shake my head.

"*No!* We can do that tomorrow. Let's try to get a lift. Where are we going now? It must be late at night and it is not safe to go home."

Tears are creeping out the corners of my eyes. I am exhausted. The fire must have taken a bit more out of me than I thought. Now I am in the fresh air I just want to go to sleep somewhere safe.

"I can only think of one place to go. Let's go to the office. I have no idea how to get there though. Who would want to give a lift to anyone dressed like you at this time of night?"

We hurry as fast as we can until we are a few streets away from the police compound so no one will be looking for us out here. I glare at Stuart and stick out my thumb as I walk up the street. Soon a car pulls over.

"Can you take us into town, please?" I ask the old man at the wheel.

He looks at me and Stuart then smiles.

"You are going to a fancy dress party, aren't you? I used to love those when I was young. I know who you are pretending to be! You are dressed as that reporter Stella.....Sylvia.... yes that is her name, Sylvia Stark. You sound just like her! Come on, get in!" He laughs as we get in his car.

"You must be her camera man she is always having fights with. I love watching her. She is so funny without trying."

Stuart gets in the front so I can wiggle into the back and spread my legs wide to take the pressure off the bandages and the burns.

How embarrassing! One of my fans thinks he recognises me looking like this.

As soon as we are in his car and driving away, Stuart talks to Andy about the latest cricket and footy matches while I relax into the seat and think about our escape.

There is something about the figure who rescued us that I can't put my finger on. I was so sure it was Harold Dumpt at the time as he was the one I was expecting. But was it? I can't be sure. His voice was muffled and indistinct.

Sitting silently in the back of the car, putting distance between us and the prison we were held in, I look forward to being able to talk to Stuart about his observations.

Until then I don't want Andy to know it is really me.

Finally standing on the street corner in town in the middle of the night, the realization of our escape hits us. It is not safe to go home but are we really going to be safe in the office?

As we walk to the News building the questions finally start pouring out of me.

"How did Dumpt disappear like that? How did he know where to find us? Why did he rescue us? Was it really him?"

Stuart nods in agreement. "I am asking myself those same questions!"

"Do you think he is employed by the King or by Fairy Godmothers?" I ask but not really expecting an answer.

"Maybe both."

I look at him for a moment as a light bulb goes off in my head!

"Is that the wall he was sitting on? He wanted to be on both sides at the same time? If that is the case, no wonder he fell."

It is really creepy going in to the office as the clock on the wall strikes Two o'clock in the Morning. I have never been here so late or early. I feel as if I am breaking in even though we have the password for the electronic keypad. Besides being wrapped up like a half fried mummy and dressed in a large floral sack that reaches nearly to my ankles doesn't do a lot for my image either.

"We need to write down as much information as we can," Stuart says softly, relocking the door behind us.

"We also need to make sure someone knows about what is going on under the Police compound in case we disappear again."

"Don't turn the lights on," I warn him as we make our way to my desk. "We don't want to let anyone know we are here.

If the police come to check out who is here this late they may take us back to the dungeon."

Okay, that may be a feeble excuse but it is the best I can come up with this time of night. I don't want to see myself in any reflections just yet. I can tell my hair is a mess by feeling it.

Silently I turn on my computer and quickly type everything Stuart has discovered while I was stuck in bed.

All this does is add more questions to my already growing list. Why were we held like that? Was it to draw Humpty Dumpty out of hiding? Why did he rescue us?

For that matter, why did he agree to an interview in the beginning only to refuse to answer most of the questions?

"Do you think Mr Dumpt is a spy who is being blackmailed?" I ask thoughtfully as I pause in my typing to look over the list again.

Stuart stops pacing around and looks at me. "Why would he be blackmailed?"

"Remember Humpty Dumpty had a great fall. He must have found something as a spy but couldn't report it for some reason. Maybe he found out the truth behind Fairy Godmothers?"

Stuart sits next to me and looks at me carefully.

"Go ahead. Explain why you think that."

"Well, it makes sense. Smith asked me if I had heard of Fairy Godmothers. Then he said Dumpt works for them. I can see now he was fishing."

Stuart waits for me to continue.

"Fairy Godmothers works for people who want to make sure their partners are not cheating on them, right? They use spies and eavesdropping bugs, correct?"

He nods in agreement.

"What if Dumpt was working for them and found one of the Royal's was cheating on another? What if he was also working for the King and then he found out the truth about Ella? He couldn't report it to the King."

"He must be working for the King in order for him to try to come to his rescue," Stuart suggests.

"But if he was working for the King then who did he fall in front of?"

We reach the same conclusion at the same time.

"The Wicked Stepmother!"

"Does that mean he knows about the sexy parties being held at the old house?" he asks.

"Did he try to tell the King but instead Charlotte and Ella teamed up to stop him? As soon as they pulled their dress orders from his shop, he came to a fall. Just like the Prince said."

Suddenly it makes sense.

"He isn't a code breaker! What a laugh! He really is a dress maker! He must have gone to the house for a fitting and discovered what was going on."

Stuart shakes his head in frustration.

"No, he isn't just a dressmaker. How did he manage to get us out of the dungeon tonight? Those locks are electronic and only a skilled thief, locksmith or codebreaker could work them out."

"Oh." I am even more confused than normal now. "What do we really know about Humpty Dumpty?"

"Nothing other than he sat on a wall, had a great fall and the King is involved," Stuart says softly.

Suddenly the loneliness in the dark office building seems overwhelming. I look around nervously. Is someone else here?

CHAPTER THIRTY SEVEN

When the Chief arrives in the morning I am sure he is surprised to see Stuart and I sound asleep, spread out on the lounge chairs in the lunch room. The reason I am sure of it is because he stood in the one spot and didn't say anything.

Not giving his own opinion on something is extremely hard for Harry so the shock was probably deep enough to cause a heart attack. Then he left us sleep and took his coffee into his office to wait until we woke in our own time.

Totally unheard of.

It is mid morning by the time I open my eyes to the smell of a fresh cup of coffee wafting under my nose.

The staff room only has instant but my overstressed brain just says *'caffeine'* without any stipulations such as freshly ground, café latte, long black or whatever other variety of coffee there is.

Stuart is holding the cup in front of me and smiling.

"Wake up, Sleeping Beauty. You are late for work."

My sleep deprived brain tries to work out what is going on. What is Stuart doing in my room? Where am I? I start to jump up from the couch when I remember where I am so I snuggle back down again.

"Nope, I was extra early today."

"Time to get up!" he says more firmly. "There is work to be done."

I look around the room and frown. Why are all the mirrors covered?

I look again at Stuart and he is trying to keep from laughing. Oh Boy! I must look really bad. I haven't had my makeup kit for a week.

"The Chief wants us to come to his office as soon as you are awake enough," he says as he returns to the bench and puts a couple of pieces of bread in the toaster.

"How is your wife?" I ask, sipping on the caffeine potion that tastes like the most delicious dirty dish water I have ever had. "Did you get through to her?"

Stuart nods as he looks through the fridge for some more food.

"Yes, she managed to get away and is safely out of town."

I can hear the relief in his voice. He must have been very worried over the last few days.

"Here," he says putting two pieces of toast with cheese in front of me. "I've already eaten. Take this and let's go."

"Should I go tidy up first?" I ask as I get up and rearrange my granny pyjamas.

I put my hands up to straighten my hair but it is brittle and frizzy, beyond repair. Maybe that is why he covered the mirrors.

"We don't have time," he says as he hurries me out the door. "We want to get to his office before the other reporters arrive from their first interviews."

"Why?"

"Let's just say you are looking .... Different to your normal radiant self."

Frowning with frustration at being rushed, I walk stiff legged into the Chief's office. I am going to have to remove the bandages as soon as possible. Hopefully the new skin will be okay after all the lotion and gel that has been put on it.

"Sylvia, how are you feeling?" Harry asks, clearly concerned about my welfare.

I look between the two men watching me carefully then march up to the window to see my reflection. It is not very clear but I can see enough to know it is not good.

My hair is ruined and mostly black.

Putting my hand to my face, I can feel what they are so worried about.

I am peeling! I look like I have leprosy!

The lotions in the dungeon must have been holding the itch and peel at bay but now it has dried it is starting to come loose.

Tears spring to my eyes as I silently return to my chair and nibble on the toast.

"Are you okay?" Harry asks again as he comes around his desk and squats down next to my chair.

"I am ugly," I whisper tearfully.

"You could never be ugly, Sylvia. You are just not as gorgeous as you normally are. Just wait until my wife gets here. I have asked her to go to your house and bring some clothes for you as well as your make up kit. She is a hair dresser, you know. She will have your hair back to ..... maybe not normal but it will be better than it is now."

Tears are streaming down my face as I look up at Stuart and Harry. I must look pathetic but I really don't care. I am not used to getting kidnapped and..... sniff, sniff.

"What do you want us to do?" Stuart asks Harry. "We have obviously upset someone."

"I want you to interview Dumpt's neighbours, Charlotte Johansson and even go back and speak to Dumpt himself if you can," he says making his way back to his desk.

"I want to kidnap Officer Smith!" I say firmly.

My anger at what has happened is starting to rise and dry my tears. I lift up my head to look at the two men standing next to the desk. Stuart and Harry look at me in surprise. Smiles start to creep over their faces as they think my suggestion through.

"What a good idea! Fight unfair with unfair! This time you are in the position of power. He will think you are running and hiding and never suspect you to come after him," Harry says, picking up his pad of paper.

Then in typical 'Chief' style he continues. "This is the way I think you should go about it."

CHAPTER THIRTY EIGHT

By the time Susie Parker has finished doing her magic with scissors on my hair and applying layers of makeup, Stuart has removed the paper from off the mirrors. A few other staff members have arrived in the office but they are kept away from where I am being looked after.

Cautiously I walk up to one of the mirrors to check out the damage.

Eeek!

Who is that?? I jump back in surprise. Oh, it is me.

I have never had such short hair before. I touch it and smooth the soft tight blonde curls in place. Not bad, I guess. I tuck the curls behind my ears but they are too short to stay there.

Actually I look a bit more sophisticated than I normally do. Maybe people won't think I am so dense now my hair looks like it is controlled in this trendy cut. I have never been able to understand how hair can make such a difference.

Of course not having any at all would not be a good look unless it is for a cause like a cancer fund raising appeal. Maybe

I should try that? I wonder how I would look without any hair at all? No, I am not that brave yet.

Next I look closely at my face. The skin is peeling pretty badly but the foundation is holding it in place. My sunglasses had protected my eyes so I must look like a white and red raccoon with leprosy without the foundation.

Dressed in one of my comfortable royal blue pantsuits, I nod with satisfaction.

Yep. I am not beaten. I will not shrink into a heap! I will rise from the ashes like a Phoenix! That is one of those birds with large claws that come out of a fire, I think. Anyway, I will rise!

Before I start making faces at myself in the mirror, I turn to find Stuart smiling at me.

"Wow!" he exclaims. "You look different. Much better."

"Thanks. Now let's get to work and find out what Humpty Dumpty is really up to."

Soon we are outside Mr Dumpt's house, watching for any sign of someone being home. We only escaped last night so I am still a little nervous that one of Smith's men might be watching the house as well.

"I am going to speak to the neighbours. You stay here." Stuart says softly.

"I want to go too," I protest but I make no attempt to get out of the car.

I am still feeling a bit 'fragile'. I like that word 'fragile'. It can mean a lot of different things. It can mean weak like a tissue or it can mean precious like a Ming vase. I prefer to think of myself as a delicate Ming vase but at the moment tissues are coming in handy as my eyes keep leaking.

No, I am not crying. I am a Phoenix!

"Someone wants you dead," he replies firmly, pulling me back down to reality. "I want to prevent that."

As soon as he leaves I sink down in the seat so that no one will be able to see me if they are driving past. It is actually really comfortable snuggling in like this. I could easily fall to sleep here and no one would see me.

"Have you seen anything?" he asks as he opens the door suddenly.

Oops! I must have nodded off.

"I thought I was supposed to stay safe and out of sight," I reply, smiling brightly as I wiggle my way back into the seat.

A good hour's sleep has definitely improved my mood.

"Well, while you were hiding I have spoken to the most boring neighbours a person could have. They don't even know the Dumpt's. There is never anything strange going on, no cars coming or going other than them going to work each day, nothing."

I struggle to sit up straight. "How can he be a dress maker if he doesn't have deliveries? Maybe he has a shop somewhere? Should we check that out next?"

"Do you still think he is a dressmaker?" he asks. "I thought we agreed he was a spy."

"Maybe his wife is the dress maker?" I suggest.

"That is a possibility. I think we need to go talk to him now. He must realise we will come see him when we can."

I nod and prepare to get out of the car. "Let's do it, Sherlock."

I barely knock on the door when it opens and we are hurried inside.

"Come in," Mr Dumpt says grabbing my arm and pulling me inside. "I have been waiting for you ever since you pulled up to spy on me."

"We want to thank you for rescuing us," I say as I follow him into his lounge room.

With the pants on I am able to walk normally without the skin rubbing together so the bandages are much smaller. Blister on blister is simply too much pain to describe.

Mrs Dumpt comes out of the kitchen and hobbles over to the lounge to sit next to her husband as before.

"What happened to your ankle?" I ask.

"I tripped over something and twisted it," she chuckles. "It happens all the time."

"I am sorry to hear that," I reply as a huge question mark appears inside my head.

I wonder if she......?

Two hours later we are back outside the Dumpt's house and my head is spinning. As soon as we told him the Prince had actually spoken to us, he opened up and explained everything.

Now we have to rewrite the Nursery Rhyme.

Humpty Dumpty climbed up a wall
Humpty Dumpty sat nice and tall
All the king's horses and all the king's men
Didn't need to put Humpty together at all.

"Okay," Stuart says as he starts to car and heads back towards the office. "That was enlightening even though it wasn't what we expected. How do you want to do the next part? How are we going to kidnap a corrupt police detective?"

"Could we just ask him to come for a drive with us?"

He looks at me and shakes his head.

"How about we give him some of the treatment he gave us?"

"*No!* You can't bomb his house! That is illegal. He might get hurt." I gasp.

"I was thinking about what he did to me. Although he didn't seem too worried about what effect his bomb may have had on you. Admittedly it was only a very small one, but I can see you are still in a lot of pain," Stuart replies gently.

"The lotion helps," I say as I take out a tube and spread it on an itchy spot on my face. "I can't understand why Officer Smith would arrange for the black hummer gang to herd us into the Police compound and to set the bomb in my garage."

I lean back in the seat and work through what we have found out so far.

Harold Dumpt claims he is just a dressmaker but for some reason people think he knows more than he does because of his nickname. He has his theories but until we get it confirmed from Smith himself, he doesn't want to say any more other than he knows there is corruption in the Secret Service and Smith is deep in the thick of it.

He didn't think the Fairy Godmothers was behind the hummer gang and our kidnapping but Officer Smith is tied up with them somewhere along the way.

What I still don't know is Why? Why come after us?

"Should we talk to Charlotte Johansson before we kidnap Smith?" I ask Stuart as he pulls into the local hardware shop's car park.

"No. The plan is to get him to talk and then use what he says to present to Charlotte. Maybe she will back off from Dumpt then."

"Harold never said why she is after him other than thinking he has information he claims not to have and we know Smith is after him. Don't you find that strange? How do we know if he is telling the truth? Charlotte must have something over him to be blackmailing him into keeping his silence and not telling us what is really going on. How does he get his information? It seems others can't work out if he is a spy or dressmaker either."

"I don't understand how the espionage industry works," Stuart admits. "However, he did come rescue us."

"Did he? That is another thing he didn't really answer. I find it all confusing like someone is not telling us the truth. If it was him that rescued us, how did he know? He must have been told to by the King. How did the King know we were kidnapped?"

"I don't know but by the time we are finished with Smith hopefully we will have more of an idea of the answers to those questions."

I start giggling as soon as Stuart returns with the ropes, duct tape and cable ties.

"I will finally have a captive audience to ask my questions to. He won't be able to escape without answering them. Maybe we can finally get complete answers instead of all this confusion."

CHAPTER THIRTY NINE

It is late in the evening when Stuart and I arrive at the spot where we plan to ambush Officer Smith.

We are both dressed in black pants and black long sleeved shirts.

As we see his car turn onto the road, we pull on our black balaclavas. I must say, we look like some real bad dudes. At least, Stuart does. I don't think 'real bad dudes' are supposed to have a case of the giggles. I can't help it.

I have to do a mad dash across the road like I am out of control! I am so well practiced at mad dashes while trying to get a parking spot at the supermarket this is going to be *fun*!

I put on my best 'bad dude' look as I jump into the driver's seat of the black van we hired and plant my foot heavily on the accelerator. The vehicle jumps with excitement and leaps like a panther, dashing across the road and nearly crashing into Officer Smith's sedan as he comes up next to me. Then I spin the wheel and come up perfectly behind him.

Smith pulls wildly on the steering wheel to avoid the collision and his car jumps up the curb, along the footpath and hits a big tree. Steam comes pouring out of his radiator.

Oops!

"Stupid Woman Driver!" Smith yells out the window.

He gets out, fuming, looking from his damaged car then around to see where I have ended up.

Huh! This 'stupid woman driver' has nicely pulled up right behind him without a single scratch to my car. So *who* is the bad driver?

I can see he is ready to tear me apart as he advances towards my door.

Before he can reach me, Stuart comes behind him, knocks him to the ground and puts a rope around him like one of those rodeo cowboys. I jump out with the duct tape in one hand and get to work securing a bag over his head.

Meanwhile Stuart holds him face down and secures his arms. He is fighting but we are too good. Too smooth. Too lucky.

Within a minute of my mad dash across the road, we have his hands cable tied, his mouth and feet thoroughly duct taped and the bag secured over his head. I feel like doing a high-five! My first kidnapping! What a buzz!

The one problem with being so overly zealous with the duct tape is now he is laying on the ground thoroughly tied up and he can't walk. Stuart looks at me but doesn't say anything. I know what he is thinking though. Oops!

"Get up!" Stuart growls angrily in Smith's ear as he grabs his arm and rolls him over.

I look at him in surprise. I have never heard him speak like that. If I could get up from where I am standing, I would obey pretty quickly. Smith is trying to talk. I am sure he is complaining about his legs being taped together.

"Hop!" I demand in the nastiest voice I can.

It doesn't sound nearly as threatening as Stuart's but I am pretty pleased with my attempt. He hops while Stuart and I guide him into the car. Carefully I put the seat belt around him then push him over so he is lying on his side.

"Stay."

Stuart and I jump into the front seat of the van and look at each other, trying not to laugh. We just kidnapped a police officer!

We agreed not to talk while we have our victim in the car so silently Stuart drives to the house in the country that the Chief had suggested.

It is a small house that looks like it was built a long time ago. I wonder how Harry knew about this place?

I wonder if a Fairy Tale started here once upon a time? It looks like a cottage from Little Red Riding Hood's time period.

As soon as we arrive, we help Smith get out and he hops inside.

I can imagine how hard it must be to hop without being able to see where you are going so I am tempted to give it a try.

One look at Stuart puts that thought out of my mind, so I turn on the lights. Finally we have Smith sitting in a spare empty room, tied to a chair with a rope. I have wrapped him up like a giant spider has secured him for his next dinner but I still am not sure if he will escape.

"Shall I duct tape him to the chair?" I ask softly.

Stuart raises his eyebrows and shakes his head. "He is not going anywhere. Don't overdo it."

I slump my shoulders and put the duct tape back in the bag. Spoil Sport!

"Now what?" I ask. "Do we take off our disguises?"

"I guess so," he says. "I never thought about what happens now. As soon as we do there is no going back. We will be wanted felons."

I take off my balaclava and run my fingers through my short curls.

"I want him to know he can't get away with kidnapping us."

I walk up to Smith and remove the bag then rip the tape off his mouth. I am sure it hurt but so did the burns. I am almost tempted to stick some tape on his arms to let him know how much it hurt.

Yes, I am being a little sadistic but as long as someone else is suffering the pain I am okay with that.

I gasp at the thought. What has come over me?! Has the fire turned me into Dr Jekyll or Mr Hyde?

"*You!*" he exclaims angrily. "What do you think you are doing? It is a federal felony to kidnap a police officer."

"Oh Yeah!" I say cheekily in his face. He can't hurt me now!

"We did and so what?! What are you going to do about it? Besides, what you did to me is one as well, so there. We're even."

"You will be sorry," he lowers his voice and growls.

I step back and look around for Stuart. Stuart steps forward and slaps Smith across the face.

"You better mind your manners. If you don't answer the questions you won't be going anywhere except six feet under."

Smith looks shocked by the treatment and the threat. Six feet under? Are we going to kill him? That wasn't part of the plan. I sure hope Stuart is just trying to scare him. It seems to have worked as his shoulders slump.

"What do you want to know?" he asks a bit more humbly.

"I want to know why you are out to destroy Mr Dumpt?" I ask, sitting in a chair facing him as if it is a normal interview.

"Why do you think I want to destroy him?"

"You said you wanted to trap him. You wanted to use us as bait to catch him but he managed to slip past you anyway," I reply then I stop as I realise what is happening. I want him to give us the information, not for me give it to him.

"Just answer the question."

He sighs deeply then seems resolved to the fact he has no choice. He is a captive audience.

"Humpty Dumpty is a code name for a very clever code breaker who has been able to find secrets the Secret Service has kept well hidden from anyone."

"Suddenly the King knows what we are up to and I get called in to answer questions. I have been trying to find out who it is. Once upon a time I was so sure it was Dumpt that I had him arrested and raided his house but I found nothing."

"Why do you think he is a code breaker? He is just a dress maker."

Oops, I am going it again.

"A dress maker?" Smith exclaims. "Why would a dressmaker use codes?"

"Maybe they are not codes. Maybe what you are looking at is measurements for a dress pattern or something?" I suggest.

"No, I found this Humpty Dumpty had infiltrated the Fairy Godmother's spy agency and reported back to the King."

"What did he report?"

"I don't actually know. All I know is the King told the Prince who told the Princess who told the Wicked Stepmother who runs the agency."

"And?" I prompt.

"The Fairy Godmother withdrew from a number of jobs. They were clearly afraid of what he had found."

"Why are you interested in what they are doing? Are you a double agent?"

Stuart looks at me in surprise. It had just occurred to me so why not ask? We had thought Dumpt was a double agent. It now appears he is only working for the King.

Smith doesn't want to answer at first then he nods his head.

"Yes, I get a few jobs from them every now and then. It is mainly when they find someone who is doing something illegal. I go in undercover and gather the evidence then make the arrest."

So, Officer Smith is working for Fairy Godmothers. Is that corrupt? Maybe or maybe not.

"Let me get this straight. You bombed my house and kidnapped us so you could trap the elusive Humpty Dumpty when he came to rescue us. How did you know he was going to come get us?"

"I reported what you told me to the King. When you 'disappeared' I told him where I thought you might be."

"Why didn't you catch him then?"

"It wasn't him who came for you. I had men watching his house the whole time and he never left except to go to a shop in town. My men watched him the whole time."

"But it had to be him!" I protest.

In the back of my mind, I am trying to recall what he had said when we spoke to him during our rescue. His voice was muffled.

Suddenly I realise I couldn't be sure if it really was him. When we spoke to him at his house we had already assumed it was him so we never actually asked the right question. I wonder who it was?

Smith looks at me surprised then shakes his head sadly.

"It wasn't him."

"What about the great fall? How could that fit if Dumpt is a spy?"

"All I know is Humpty Dumpty hasn't been doing any reporting lately," he says, shrugging his shoulders.

"There hasn't been a leak for the last year but I still want to stop him from breaking into our systems."

"Mr Brown said Dumpt took a fall when his dress making business was forced to change. It appears whatever he reported resulted in all the dress orders for the Royal family being withdrawn, sending him nearly broke."

Officer Smith shakes his head emphatically. "No, No, that cannot be the truth. Surely I haven't spent years chasing a dress maker!"

I chuckle at his distress. I know it is cruel but he deserves it.

"Yep. That is what it looks like. I want to ask why you had us harassed by the black hummer?"

"In the first case, Fairy Godmothers needed you to back off the Princess. I knew if you got her riled up the court case could expose everything. Thankfully she handled it perfectly and kept most of the truth secret. This last time, I needed you to trust me to tell me what you had found. The hummer herded you straight to my waiting arms."

"Why did I get shot?" Stuart asks angrily.

"I wanted you to back off so the shot was meant to scare you off. You weren't supposed to get hit."

"Any idea what the information may have been that turned the Fairy Godmothers against Dumpt's dressmaking?" Stuart asks.

Hadn't I asked that before?

"No," Smith answers, his shoulders slumped. "All I know is someone is telling the King information we don't want him knowing just yet. I am going to have to go back to looking at the members of my old team. I was so sure it wasn't any of them."

"Okay. I am finished asking questions," I say, standing up and preparing to leave the room.

"You kidnapped me for that?! I would have spoken to you privately if you had just asked. Oh, except I guess you didn't trust me anymore. What are you going to do with me now?" he asks nervously.

"We thought we might give you what you deserve," I giggle. "You have wanted a chance to talk to Humpty Dumpty so he is going to look after you now. Just be careful what you say. He might decide to take your measurements for a comfy wooden box."

I walk up close enough behind him to whisper in his ear without him being able to grab me. Finally I get to say the line I have been wanting to.

"Watch your back."

Stuart leaves the room and returns with Harold Dumpt. He is dressed in black and looks really dangerous.

"I plan to take you for a little drive," he says in his thick accent. "By the time I am through you will not harass me or my family anymore."

Smith's face loses its colour as Dumpt removes the duct tape binding his ankles and forces him to stand.

"Take care, Officer Smith. It has been nice having a chat," I giggle nervously.

Stuart shakes his head as he looks at me. He does that a lot I have noticed. I start to giggle more and more. Okay, I am getting a little hysterical now. I have just kidnapped a police officer and handed him over to ......a deadly spy or a dressmaker.

"Stuart, what is Mr Dumpt? A spy or a dressmaker?"

"I still think he is both."

"I am beginning to think Mrs Dumpt is more to be reckoned with."

"What do you mean?"

"The rhyme never says Humpty Dumpty is a man. Camilla could be the spy."

"Do you really think so? She is so short and round it is hard to believe she could run like the person who rescued us."

"I wonder if that is part of her disguise? Maybe she was wearing one of those fat suits under her dress when we saw her. She could get to all the ladies parties and fit right in. The best sources of information are these gossip sessions."

"Possibly," he finally admits. "We will have to wait to see what Charlotte has to say next."

It takes a couple of weeks before the Chief is happy to let me out in the public's eye again.

In the meantime I am stuck at my desk writing articles and doing phone interviews for the Celebrity News. It is not nearly as exciting as being out in the field and in front of the camera but having great sheets of skin peeling off me is not exactly attractive. By the time I am able to leave the office, I have gone full circle again.

Maybe Officer Smith and I are looking for something that is not there?

The only unexplained thing is that Stuart and I were rescued by someone good with electronic locks.

That anomaly is the only thing keeping me from concluding Harold Dumpt is simply a dressmaker.

CHAPTER FORTY

Our final interview for the case is with Charlotte Johansson.

I can't get my head around how someone can be the Fairy Godmother and yet the Wicked Stepmother at the same time.

When I first spoke to her she had been so sweet and grandmotherly but after she got the *huge* compensation for the slander she had to undergo for so many years, she had shown her true colours.

We had been friends until then. I am still a little hurt by the sudden cutting off, after all the support I had given her.

I am still getting letters from the Stepmothers support group I helped establish during the court case.

Okay, I admit I feel really hurt by her cutting off. Maybe that is the reason she got the label of 'Wicked'. Anyway, now I have to face her again I am very apprehensive.

"You will be fine," Stuart says reassuringly as we sit in front of her house in the trendy suburb of Daydreams, back where it all began. "Do you have your list of questions ready?"

"Sort of…. Well, actually, no," I admit. "I am having trouble concentrating so I haven't got them as organised as I should have."

Instead of mocking me or smirking as he normally would, Stuart looks at me with a serious, concerned expression on his face. I am worried about myself as well. I have lost my flippantness, my confidence to breeze through an interview. I wonder what was in that bomb? Was there a potion in it to make me wake up to the real dangers of life?

I am not so sure I want to know the truth about anything anymore.

"Let's do this," I say, plastering on a smile and glancing in the rear view mirror to make sure my makeup and hair is in place.

I am not used to having hair not much longer than Stuart's but it definitely has its advantages. Maybe that is why I don't feel flippant anymore? Maybe I am like Samson of the Bible? Cut my hair and I lose my sense of humour. After all, wasn't that my strength?

Sighing deeply I step out of the car and walk to the front door.

"Don't worry about the camera. Just use your little recorder thingy."

Stuart's mouth drops open in surprise as I shrug my shoulders. So what? I don't need a camera in my face all the time. It has been nice having a break from plastering a smile on and playing up to the invisible audience.

It has been a long time since we were last here. I knock on the door three times and feel a twinge. Is that my humour coming back? I look around half expecting Stuart to have the huge black camera case on his shoulder. A real smile lights my face. Am I returning to old myself?

The butler answers the door and hesitates for a moment before he welcomes us inside and leads us to the sitting room we have been in many times before. I am always amazed by the warm colours and inviting furniture in this room. The grandeur of the outside doesn't give that feeling of warmth and homeliness like the sitting room does.

When Charlotte enters the room she is surprised to see me but as always she manages to hide it well.

"Welcome, my dears! It has been so long since we have had a chance to chat. Please sit down."

As soon as we are seated, the butler returns with cups of tea and homemade cookies. That was quick. Had they expected us?

"I am sorry for not keeping in touch," she says softly as she sits down and makes herself comfortable. I almost believe she means it. "I have been so busy."

"I am sure you have," I reply with a touch of sarcasm.

Yep, busy arranging for the hummer to harrass us and Smith to kidnap us. Yep, very busy. Actually I shouldn't assume it was her that arranged that. Maybe Officer Smith took it on himself as his role in the Secret Service. All these double agents! Ugh! I don't know who is working for who. It almost seems immoral.

"What is the matter? You look sad, Sylvia dear. Don't you like your new hair cut?"

I jerk my head in surprise. How does she know about my hair cut? Oh, of course. She can see it.

"A lot has happened since we spoke. I am sorry but this is not the time to chat. I have come to ask you a few questions, Charlotte. Off the record of course," I say, picking up the cup of tea.

"I have been looking into the Nursery Rhyme of Humpty Dumpty. Are you familiar with it?"

"Yes, of course," she laughs but the humour doesn't reach her eyes.

"I understand Mr Harold Dumpt was in your employ before he was dumped. What can you tell us about the circumstances?"

She raises her eyebrows and thinks for a moment. "Off the record?"

"Yes, I have already said that."

"Mr Dumpt was our dressmaker. You remember my telling you how I bought a new dress for the girls as they got bigger? Well, after Ella married the Prince and the Cinderella story came out, we had no need for fancy dresses any more".

"All invitations vanished into thin air. Antoinette and Gabriella left home soon after that so I cancelled any further gowns. I believe Ella may have decided to cut all ties with her former life and that included the dress maker. As soon as word got out the Princess was no longer using him, I suppose everyone thought something was wrong with the quality of his gowns. Misinformation can be so cruel."

She sighs before she continues.

"I felt really bad for the way he was treated but there was nothing I could do about it."

"So you are saying, he is really a dressmaker?"

"Yes, as far as I am aware. Why do you ask? Did you expect something else?"

"Well, yes actually." I glance at Stuart.

Should I divulge the information we have? He is concentrating on picking out one of the delicious looking cookies on the plate. No help coming from him.

"Please, Sylvia. We are friends. Surely you can trust me," Charlotte smiles as she reaches out for my hand. I take her hand and give it a little squeeze. Can I trust her?

"Okay, I have been led to believe Mr Dumpt is a spy."

"A spy? That is absurd!"

"I thought so too. We have been led to believe you employed him to spy on someone and he had to decide whether to relay it back to the King or keep it confidential and for Fairy Godmothers ears only."

She sits back in her chair as she thinks about what I am saying.

"Please continue."

"We spoke to an Officer Smith who has been trying to find out what the information was so he can arrest Mr Dumpt."

I pause for a moment.

"This is where it gets confusing. Smith says he also works for you and Fairy Godmothers at times and because of what Dumpt found you pulled out of several jobs."

"I fear Officer Smith has misunderstood the situation." She chuckles.

"All that I told you before happened at the same time as the wedding so it was many years ago as you know. I pulled out of the jobs because I had lost one of my girls and my reputation was taking a hammering. I had to lay several people off for a while. Camilla Dumpt was one of them."

"It had nothing to do with any information we had gained as he seems to believe."

"Camilla Dumpt worked for you?"

"Yes, she used to go to all the social gatherings and listen to the gossip. If something came up, she would report it back to me."

"And you dumped her because.....?" I ask, wanting her to repeat her explanation. Something is not right here.

"I had to cancel her work contract as I was downsizing the company. I needed professional agents who could gather more sensitive information. I believe she was keeping busy helping her husband in his business after that. I really don't know."

"So, Mr Dumpt is just a dressmaker?"

"I am afraid so." She stands up to leave. "I am sorry I can't give you any more time. Next time please make an appointment so I can schedule a longer chat."

CHAPTER FORTY ONE

As we sit in the office building's car park, I lean against the head rest to stop my head from spinning. I feel so disappointed to find, after all our effort and research, Mr Dumpt is only a dressmaker. That one anomaly of our rescue will just have to go away with no explanation. Stuart must be feeling the same way as he sits silently resting his head on the steering wheel.

"What did Mr Dumpt say while we were at his house the last time?" he asks after a few minutes.

"He spoke about the drop in his work. I was so sure it was code for spying," I reply softly. "I guess I read too much into the simple nursery rhyme from the beginning."

"Maybe."

Suddenly a light bulb comes on in my head.

"*Whoa*! Wait a minute! We forgot to ask Charlotte who Humpty Dumpty was!"

"I doubt she knows. She only knew about the dressmaking side."

"Oh, yeah, I forgot." I rest back, still puzzled by the flash bulb that is flickering in my mind. It has to do with that name.

"Charlotte didn't comment on the reason we thought Dumpt was a spy. She just skirted around it."

Stuart waits for me to continue.

"You know what? It has been in front of us all the time!" I laugh with a touch of hysteria. "Camilla is the egg shaped one. She is always falling over, remember? She is the one that was on the wall, not her husband."

Stuart looks at me, frowning.

"Keep going."

"Harold is a dressmaker, right? We have established that fact by speaking to the Prince and to Charlotte. No one ever said anything about his wife other than she worked for Charlotte for awhile. She is never referred to as another dressmaker."

"Yeeeessss, so?"

"Remember, she was the one to explain how the King's horses and the King's men meant the King's wealth and his influence. She sounded like someone who really knew what she was talking about. I wondered why she would have to explain it if Harold was the spy. That is because *she* is the spy! It was her that rescued us. When she ran off in the dark she must have sprained her ankle then."

"What would she have found that caused the fall in the rhyme?"

"Maybe nothing. Maybe it is not related, just like Harold said. He took the fall with his business going poorly after Ella got married and cut ties with her past."

I am starting to get excited now. I can see how several pieces finally are starting to fit together.

"Camilla.....if her name is misspelt or said with a thick accent it sounds like Camel. A camel has humps.....Humpty! Camilla aka Humpty Dumpty is the double agent. She worked for the King and for Fairy Godmothers. She must have found out about the sexy lingerie parties that are being held at the old house and thought Ella was being disloyal to the Prince."

"She had to decide whether to tell the King or stay silent to keep her employment with Fairy Godmothers. She would have told the King who must have thought it was important enough to tell the Prince who then turned around and told Ella."

"Maybe the Prince was involved in it as well? Instead of stopping her activities, she withdrew her dress orders, knowing it would hurt both the Dumpts. Remember it happened just after they got married so she would have needed a whole new wardrobe. The order would have been huge."

Stuart nods and waits for me to think it through.

"Harold Dumpt said his business took a hammering but he changed into a different field making men's suits. So his business took a turn, not a fall."

"However, Camilla lost her job with Fairy Godmothers, not because of the downturn but they found out she had broken the confidentiality clause. That would be the fall."

"Harold even hinted at it when he gave the illustration of the powerful politician who was caught and fell from his position. Instead it was his wife. If she had been exposed the politician taking the fall would have been the King. Because of this confidentiality clause, the King could not interfere."

"She had been a secret agent so that the King can get to know what is really going on in his realm. Maybe she still is. Smith was sure angry some of their secrets got out. I wonder how she got them?"

"He said Humpty Dumpty is a code breaker so the information must be encrypted. Maybe someone in the Secret Service has been giving the secrets to her camouflaged as dress measurements? She must have some equipment in the house so she can run the coded messages to decipher them."

"That makes the most sense otherwise she has to be a master Computer Hacker as well."

I take a deep breath and prepare to get out of the car to return to the office. We need to get this written up as soon as possible. Now all the pieces are neatly in place, I feel vindicated at keeping onto the case.

"So the truth is Humpty Dumpty is not a 'he' but is a 'she'. The reference to sitting on the wall must be that she has been spying on the locals to find out what is going on behind closed doors, or over walls in the local gossip sessions."

"It backfired when she reported something to do with Fairy Godmothers spy agency and that resulted in her becoming exposed. So she fell from her position and the King couldn't do anything or he would have been exposed for using a spy on his own people."

"It is one thing to spy on other countries to make sure they are not wanting to start a war with us but it is totally another to play Big Brother and spy on your own citizens. Officer Smith was already getting persistent with pursuing the leaking of information so the King had to be careful."

I nod with satisfaction. Yep, we have solved the Nursery Rhyme.

"The moral is to keep your mouth shut or you may upset someone enough to get hurt or lose your job and there is nothing anyone can do about it. And that goes for anyone no matter how tall the wall is that they may be sitting on."

Stuart laughs as we walk through the door and head for our desks.

"It is amazing how much trouble we have had finding out what a four lined nursery rhyme really means."

"It should make a good story if we are allowed to publish it," I admit. "I'll see what I can put together while you work on the camera footage. I still wonder what the information was actually about. It had to be something so serious Fairy Godmothers felt threatened. Do you think it was just the sexy lingerie party? Maybe there is something else going on? I wouldn't be surprised if it is something much more sinister than a bit of fun with the girls. I would like to dig a bit deeper and see what happens."

Just then a shout comes for the Chief's office.

"Sylvia!! Who have you upset this time? The Palace wants you on restrictions again!"

Uh Oh!

CHAPTER FORTY TWO

Being put under restriction again is supposed to make me stop, right? Wrong! It sparks my curiosity even more.

What is it about this story that has riled the Palace up enough to pull rank again? Just as well Harry doesn't like rank pulling almost as much as I don't like it.

All the clues seem to be up in the air and just out of reach of a logical explanation.

When my frustration reaches to the point I am ready to explode, it is time to go to the gym and burn some energy. I haven't done it for a long time but now I am able to walk normally it is time to see if working out clears my mind.

Besides I like to watch myself in the mirrors. Damn, I look good in tight clothes. What an ego boost!

The Kings Gymnasium is the best in town and always busy. After a brief scan to check out the guys lifting weights and making sure they notice me I head to my favourite equipment ready to burn some fat cells.

As I make my way towards the only vacant treadmill in the room, I can't help wondering what is behind this story.

Is Camilla a spy or not?

What is the information that is so important that she was willing to risk her job with Fairy Godmothers?

I have asked all the questions but nothing seems to be falling in place yet.

Deep in the back of my mind I am not convinced Camilla is the one who rescued us. Her round shape appears to be her own and not a fat suit.

As I pound away on the treadmill, slowly increasing the speed I look around at the other equipment around me. Most people have head phones plugged into their ears, zoning out of the reality of tired flesh to the beat of their favourite tunes. I don't mind as it gives me a chance to think through the situation.

An hour later, with the sweat pouring off my body, my mind hasn't come up with the solution yet. The window in front of me looks into an adjoining room where there is a rock climbing wall.

There appears to be a competition of some kind going on at the most challenging wall of all and the competitors are climbing free of any ropes. A petite woman is climbing with such skill and ease I slow down my pace to watch her. She is amazing as she climbs the steep ledges and even the ones where she is upside down with such ease she looks like she should have been born a monkey! As soon as she scales the final ledge she sits on top of the wall and celebrates.

I can just make out what is being said as a judge announces to the audience watching.

"Hayley Dumpt wins the ultimate challenge in the individual category! Humpty Dumpty wins the team round and a place in the Grand Final!"

Humpty Dumpty? Shock sweeps over me at the mention of that name. I stop walking before the treadmill comes to a complete stop, nearly falling off the edge.

Humpty Dumpty? Have I been looking in the wrong areas all together?

I make my way into the rock climbing room trying to look more casual than I feel and towards the challenge board. Immediately the names of the other teams catch my attention.

Horse Power and Army Reserves are competing against Humpty Dumpty for a position in the Grand Final and the right to represent the gym against those across the country. Last year Humpty Dumpty lost for the first time in many years. Instantly my mind starts filling in the gaps.

Humpty Dumpty sat on a wall (rock climbing)
Humpty Dumpty had a great fall (lost the number one spot)
All the Kings horses (King's gym Horse Power) *and all the Kings men* (Army reserves)
Couldn't put Humpty together again (It was a competition. They lost.)

I shake my head in dismay. After all this investigating, is this the real meaning of the rhyme? Surely not.

I walk over to the area where the teams are congregating so I can get a better look at Hayley. There is something about her that causes the hair to rise on my arms. She is wiping the sweat from her forehead when she sees me looking around for her.

Our eyes meet and at that instant I know who rescued us from the dungeon. Camilla is not the spy.

It is their daughter, Hayley!

"Interesting name for your climbing team," I say after I introduce myself and wait for her to finish drying off.

"Can I speak to you privately for a moment, Hayley?"

"Sure, let's get a drink."

We step outside the gym to the small café and order a coffee. My head is racing as I watch her elegant, well balanced movements. She has inherited her father's ability to climb anything. Does this mean there is another twist to this Nursery Rhyme?

"How did you come up with the name for your team?" I ask as we finally settle in our seats.

"It came about in a rather roundabout way. Someone wanted to call us Ups and Downs as we go up the wall then down again, then that became Humps and Dumps. Next another member decided to give it a twist so it became Humpty Dumpty."

I take a sip of my latte as I work through this new bit of information.

"That makes a good cover for your other activities then," I say softly, fishing for confirmation of my suspicions.

"I was wondering if you would work it out. Mum and Dad said you were good. So did Ella and Charlotte." She chuckles.

"My friend Princess Ella has been trying to keep her activities quiet. It is so unfair that people expect a Princess to be perfect all the time. She misses out on a lot of fun."

"Are you referring to the lingerie parties?"

"That and other things," she whispers, looking around to make sure no one can overhear us.

"I should never have told Mum where I was going that night. I should have known she would tell the King. The Prince enjoys them as well but it isn't politically acceptable."

"So are you the spy or your mother?" I am finding it a bit hard to keep up with the twists in the story.

"Which one is the code breaker the Secret service was looking for?"

"I work for the King and my mother worked for Fairy Godmothers," she sighs. "I may as well tell you the whole story. You will not stop asking questions until you find out anyway".

"I am the code breaker Humpty Dumpty. I was listening to encrypted messages from foreign countries when I discovered certain ones in the Secret Service were becoming corrupt and using that underground bunker I rescued you from to torture and interrogate people illegally so I reported it to the King. He called Officer Smith in to answer some uncomfortable questions resulting in Smith getting demoted and very angry. Afterwards Smith found out my code name and has been watching my parents but since I don't use my real surname at work I have been able to keep off his radar so far. Of course I had to change my code name all together after that."

I pass her my note pad where I have jotted my theories.

"Is all this correct then? Except it is you and not your mother."

She nods as she scans the information then hands the notepad back to me.

"You missed a couple of things. Charlotte wants to retire and move out to the country house. She needed money to renovate it so Ella arranged the compensation. I've quit working for the King and taken over Fairy Godmothers with Ella as Chief Executive Officer. Charles, Charlotte's brother is her butler".

"You will not be allowed to publish this. I would have to arrest you as a terror threat if you tell anyone, even Stuart. You will never be allowed to work in media anywhere worldwide nor get clearance for a passport or visa. There are a couple of other people I could name who are hiding in embassies around the world to keep from getting arrested by their Home Security Departments. Leaking confidential information like that is a definite threat. I can't even guess at how long of a jail sentence you would get."

I look at her stunned. She is so pretty and petite but what she is saying holds a lot of weight. I do not doubt her words for one moment.

"The public have a right to know they are being spied on. Especially now the Princess is running the agency. The King *and* the Princess both spying on the people!"

"No, the public has a right to security. If the only way to keep them safe is to spy on those in the community that would like to change that, then so be it. The ones who are not doing anything wrong have nothing to fear."

"The King focuses on National Security while Fairy Godmother's will continue the work Charlotte did. Those who use the service are grateful for the knowledge they pay for."

I sit back in my chair. My latte is finished but I wish I had an excuse to sip as I think things through.

"So how do you explain the Humpty Dumpty nursery rhyme?"

"As you may know it came out around the same time as the Cinderella story and is one reason I entered the Security work."

"Ella and I had just finished school and we came up with the initial rhyme to describe our lives."

"In life there are many ups and downs, humps and dumps. At times we may feel as secure as if we are sitting on a sturdy wall, unreachable, unbreakable or unshakeable. However in an instant that can come crashing down due to an unforeseen event whether it is an accident, trauma or terrorist activity, resulting in a painful life shattering fall. No one else can put us back together though. It is up to each one as an individual to take responsibility of our own lives and our future by stopping ourselves from continuing as a victim of our circumstances. We have to break free from the Victim mentality and become a Survivor. We have to pull ourselves back together again as no one, not the King and all his wealth or influence can do that for us."

She pauses for a moment as she thinks about she says next.

"If you want to publish that explanation you can but not how you got it or who you got it from."

I look at her, startled by her explanation.

So all my theories of spy networks and hidden agendas are just that..... theories. Oh, they can be made to fit if I twist them enough but the truth is so much more simple and it affects each one of us. And I am not allowed to publish it in all its glory!

I still need some questions answered though.

"Who sent you to rescue us?"

"Ella."

"Why?"

"She is who she is. She lost her parents at a young age even though she later found out Charlotte was her birth mother. She had a turbulent childhood in a stepfamily and although she isn't perfect she came out of it relatively unscathed. I think she handles herself well. Sure she may have done some silly things growing up but who hasn't?"

"She never stays angry for long and doesn't hold a grudge. She genuinely loves people and cares deeply about what they go through. There is a lot more than outward beauty to this girl. Overall she is just as the fairy tale describes her. She still is Cinderella to me."

Listening to Hayley as she continues to describe some of the selfless, kind acts Ella has done since she has become the Princess but made sure no one knew who was behind it brings tears to my eyes. My original definition of Cinderella comes blazing into my mind.

The lowly downtrodden young maiden who suffers the injustice of others with grace, never getting angry, always beautiful and dignified, embodying the ideal values of good, piousness and ultimate virtue.

I focus back on what Hayley is saying.

"Ella didn't expose her mother during the court case even though she could have. All this could have affected her marriage but she showed loyal love to Charlotte through all the mess. All the words and actions to the contrary were just for show. Isn't this just what you do in front of the camera?"

Hayley looks at me with a knowing look in her eyes. Yep, she has seen straight through my charade.

Finally, like a light bulb being switched on in my mind, I see the real story behind the fairy tale. It is not a matter of what is the truth in the smallest details.

The little details don't matter one iota.

It's got nothing to do with the rags to riches ideal I was focusing on in the beginning and that I thought the whole story was about.

It is about rising above difficulties and coming out the other side with your head held high. All the side issues can hide the beauty of the inner person. My investigation hasn't destroyed the fairy tale after all!

It has exposed the true value and the depth of meaning in it that has been missed for years.

Yes, *any* girl can be Cinderella if they rise above adversity without holding onto bitterness. It is in the kind and thoughtful way we treat one another regardless of any differences.

I close my notepad and stand up, eager to get back to the office and put down in writing the feeling I have at this moment.

My story is finally complete and Cinderella has been restored to her rightful place.

The truth about who Ella really is has finally been discovered and Humpty Dumpty helped me find it.